The Butcher From McGregor

Adrian Windsor

Copyright © 2019 Adrian Windsor

ISBN:978-0-9892907-8-4

Publisher:
McGregor Wood LLC
14252 Culver Dr. #352A
Irvine, CA 92604
www.adrianwindsor.com

BASED ON A TRUE STORY AS TOLD BY
RONALD KNAPP

THE NAMES HAVE BEEN CHANGED, THE
STORIES EMBELLISHED. THIS IS FICTION.

The thunder roars in huge echoing claps, and lightening flashes so intensely that it illuminates the lake below It is an violent summer storm, and the rain has been pouring down for several hours. Each flash of lightening reveals a long, private lake in Saint Jovite, at the foot of Mont Tremblant. There is a mansion at each end. The northern mansion had a bi-plane in the yard.

A dark, hulking figure is approaching the front door. He grabs the door knocker and knocks three times:

BOOM, BOOM, BOOM

BOOM, BOOM, BOOM

BOOM, BOOM, BOOM

It echoes out into the darkness and the storm. The front door of mansion opens into the foyer to a great room with a high ceiling flanked with huge mahogany beams. A heavy-set elderly woman in a long, black dress and thick black oxfords opens the door. A gravedigger stands before her. He is dressed in dripping bib overalls, rubber boots up to the thighs, covered in mud. He holds a shovel in his left hand. The thunder and lightening blast through the door, and he appears menacingly against the black sky and the rain downpour. In a loud voice, he yells, "The corpse is buried. I've come to be paid."

The woman replies, "Not tonight. Come back tomorrow." She slams the door, fighting the wind and the rain. A young man in his late 20's comes forward to comfort her. He is wearing a black suit. Under his breath he mutters, talking to himself: "All my life I wanted to kill him. They did it for me."

PART 1

Chapter 1

The brisk October air whipped around the clapboard house at 215 Chestnut Street just a few blocks from downtown Detroit so, it was easy to catch the Streetcar and get almost anywhere. The house was painted white, and it looked pretty much like every house on the block, the only distinguishing thing being the green shutters around the front window and the ivy growing up the sides of the front porch, now turned autumn red and yellow. The electrical wires, if anybody bothered to look, were a bit strange too, going up from outside the back kitchen door, up to the roof, and then across the backyard to the electrical pole. The house two doors down was wired the same way, and so was the one across the street.

Mick Clancy was no fool, and he and his buddy, Danny O'Connor, two doors down, who worked for Detroit Edison, had figured out how to wire their two houses directly to the Edison line so they wouldn't have any electric bill. They let Josie Murphy, across the street, into the scheme when he got laid off from his job at Ford Motor Company for drinking on the job. Mick knew all about drinking. When he wasn't at

Ford, you would find him with a gin bottle. He had gin bottles hidden all over the house and in the garage.

This particular October night the lights were all lit up in the bedroom his three teen-age daughters shared upstairs. Somehow Mick and Kelly Clancy had managed to fill this whole house with kids, five girls and three boys, and they were packed like sardines inside. The three boys were the oldest, early twenties, and they worked at Ford with Mick on the assembly line.

The two youngest girls were in the 4th and 6th grades, and the three oldest were all teen-agers, Kate 19, Joan 17, and Shannon 15. They were getting dressed up for a party across the bridge in Canada. They were all "lookers," especially Shannon 15, who already had round breasts protruding out from everything she wore because she only wore tight things. Joan had already tried on two skirts. They weren't quite sure what to wear.

Joan had met this guy, Frenchie, at the gas station when she was getting the car filled up. He came right up to the pump and started talking to her. He was wearing one of those cute French berets, and he had a French accent. He said he had trouble with his brakes and was waiting for the guys to fix them. Joan had only been driving a year, and everything to do with a car was strange to her, even though all the men in her house worked on cars. They only had one car, and Joan felt obligated to do a good job at the gas station since her Dad let her take it out.

Joan kind of thought Frenchie was flirting with her, and she liked it, especially his French accent. He said he was a student at Assumption College across the Bridge. Joan was impressed. No one in her family ever went to College. Then Frenchie said, "Hey, we're having a party Friday night. My buddy's parents are away, and we're going to his farmhouse just a little way from the Bridge."

Joan asked, "Could I bring my sisters?" She couldn't go alone.

Frenchie said, "Sure. Are they as good lookin' as you?"

Joan giggled. "One's even better, but a little young."

"That's ok," Frenchie said. "We'll break her in!"

He wrote down the address on a piece of paper with directions right after you get off the Bridge.

So the girls were getting dressed. The dresser in their room had a big mirror, and they took turns looking at themselves. Shannon was wearing a blouse that laced up the front and pushed out her breasts. Kate thought it was too revealing. Joan thought so, too, but she knew if she said anything, Shannon would just say she was jealous. She was jealous of Shannon. Shannon had long, red hair that flowed over her shoulders in natural curls, and her skin was totally free from the acne Joan was still fighting. And Shannon's hips were thin and Joan's were broad. And though Joan wasn't flat-chested, she was nothing compared to Shannon. Joan and Kate had the same hair – brown with a tinge of red, wavy but not curled, and certainly not red. They both had brown eyes, and Shannon had green eyes.

Everyone acknowledged Shannon was the beauty of the family, the apple of Mick's eye, and the one Kelly Clancy worried most about. Kelly entered the bedroom, sat down on the bed and watched the girls prancing and preening in front of the mirror. Kelly's auburn hair is streaked with grey. She is wearing her usual flowered house dress and oxfords. She looked Shannon up and down and said, "Shannon, you're really too young to be going to this party. You look old for your age. Joan doesn't know anything about these College boys. You are not old enough to take care of yourself."

Kate said, "Well, Ma, there are three of us. If we Clancy girls stick together, we can take care of each other.."

Joan said, "I'm driving. Shannon can sit in the back seat. We'll be all right."

Kelly Clancy had been knocked up at 14. She and Mick did nothing but have kids and more kids. Every time he stuck it in her, she got pregnant. She hoped her daughters would have a different life, not a house full of kids, tripping over hidden gin bottles. Shannon was the most head-strong of all her kids, and the most pretty. She feared for her the most. Is that what mothers are supposed to do, to be afraid? Did her poor mother, God rest her soul, have fear for her? When she found out Kelly was pregnant, she just shrugged. And then she went after Mick and grabbed him by the ear.

Within a week, they were married. Kelly had been married ever since – 25 years, 8 kids. Her body felt like a used up grocery sack, always getting emptied and then filled up. Mick wasn't a bad man. He went to work every day. She could live with the gin. It could be other women. That's what happened to her mother, God rest her soul. Kelly Clancy wondered when God would rest her soul. By golly, not before she had a good card game with her friends.

Sometimes when she was all alone, at the stove cooking stew or in the garden weeding her carrots, she would let her mind wander to the women who lived across town, on the other side of the streetcars. And she wondered what it would be like, but she only let herself go there for a little while. Father Brown said she was blessed, yes, Kelly Clancy was blessed. And she needs to go down on her knees and thank the good Lord for the house, for Ford's, for Mick, for her kids.

Kelly sat on the bed for a few minutes. The wind was howling around the window. She hoped it wouldn't be too windy on the Bridge. She was glad Joan was driving. She was more reliable than Kate. She wished some young man would take an interest in Kate – 19 already. These three teen-age girls would worry her until they were married.

Chapter 2

The 1936 blue DeSoto heads over the Ambassador Bridge. Even though it is just 8:00 p.m., it is dark. That's October in Michigan, shorter days and longer nights. The headlights penetrate the night air. Joan is driving. Kate sits beside her in the front seat. Shannon is in the back. She leans over, towards the front seat so she can hear what her sisters are saying.

"Who's going to be there?" asks Shannon.

"The boys are all students at Assumption College," says Joan. "That's really all I know. I met this guy, Frenchie, at the gas station, and he invited me to come. I asked if I could bring you two because I didn't want to come by myself. He mentioned his two friends, Jacques and Hungarian Joe. Jacques is a French name. They speak French in Canada, you know."

"Then I take it that Frenchie is yours, " observes Kate. "How many guys will be there?"

"Frenchie said about 20. There ought to be one for each of us. Who knows?"

The car draws up to a farmhouse, out in the middle of nowhere. There are cars parked all over the yard. There is only one outdoor light, up on a pole. But the lights from the house are shining through the windows of the downstairs. Each girl knows she could never go in there alone. It is too scary. None of these girls have ever been with boys.

They fantasized about it, talked at night when they were all in bed, about what it would be like to be kissed, dreamed about balls and ball gowns and Cinderella slippers. The Clancy girls are lucky to have two decent dresses. What they have going for them – they wear them well. Kelly Clancy has an eye for clothes. She always makes sure that Joan's skirts are not tight so that her bigger butt won't be noticed. Kate is the tallest, and she looks best in A-line dresses that just hang down on her and fold in around her curves. Shannon demands tight clothes, and Kelly has given in to her, all the while dreading this one will bring her trouble, probably get in trouble. Kelly knows: been there and done that.

The three girls stand outside the farmhouse door and knock. The door opens, and they are invited to come in by a young man, obviously the son of the owner of the house. He offers to take their coats. The girls look out at the fairly large living room, made to look larger because all of the furniture has been moved off to the sides to clear a space for dancing. A crank-up Victrola in the corner is playing music, and young men about 18-20 years old are hanging out in small groups, cracking jokes. A few couples dance in the middle of the room. The guys standing around are drinking Coca Cola, pouring it from green bottles and then pulling out flasks to spike it.

Joan whispers in Shannon's ear, "Don't drink anything."

A short, thin fellow with dark brown hair and brown eyes walks up to Joan and kisses her hand. That is Frenchie. He says, "I'm glad you came." He looks all three up and down, and then he asks: "Are these your sisters? You didn't tell me they are such lookers!"

Two young men, Frenchie's friends, approach the girls. One is short and chubby, with blond hair. He is awkward, like he doesn't know exactly what to do or say. He is wearing a cap and a military sort of jacket with metal buttons, a bit too tight. Frenchie introduces him as Hungarian Joe. The other young man is tall, slender, very self-confident with a big smile and cocky way about him.

Kate and Shannon thrust themselves forward, expecting to be greeted. Hungarian Joe gravitates toward Kate and asks her to dance. That leaves Shannon. The other one introduces himself: "My name is Jacques. What 's yours?" Shannon gives him a provocative wink, and says: "Shannon Clancy."

"Well, Shannon Clancy, would you like to dance.?"

Shannon moves into his open arms and says, "So glad you asked."

The couples all merge into the party. Shannon is beside herself with Joy. She nabbed the prize. Jacques speaks English with a French accent, and it literally blows her off her feet. He dances close, and she feels him breathing into her neck and ear. Jacques pulls her off to the side, pours two glasses of coke from a green bottle and pulls out a flask. Shannon remembers what Joan said, but she's too excited and wants too much to be cool, to be his girl. She takes a sip.

It's different from anything she's ever tasted before. Mick drinks his gin at home, but no one else ever has alcohol. She feels a rush around the top of her head, and she likes it. Jacques holds up his glass to click with hers. They click. Shannon drinks down the entire glass. She says, to Jacques, "Let's dance some more." Tipsy, she rises up from the chair. Jacques steadies her, holds her up. Shannon clings to him.

Jacques says, "Let's take a walk outside. You need some air." He leads her to the front door. As they go out, he puts his arm around her to protect her from the cold. "Let's go to my car so you'll keep warm." Shannon says, "Sure."

Jacques and Shannon get into the back seat of his car. He puts his arms around her and kisses her on the lips. She thinks, "It's even better than my dreams." He puts his tongue into her mouth and moves it back and forth. He kisses her on the ear. Shannon feels the twinge of excitement between her legs, before he even runs his hand up her skirt. He unlaces Shannon's top, kisses her breasts. Shannon is breathing hard. She merges into him. He puts his fingers into her crotch, begins to rub her, puts his fingers into her vagina. She trembles. He lays her down on the back seat, opens his fly, pulls out his penis, and thrusts inside her. Shannon is in ecstasy. The windows of the car are so steamed up no one can see in.

Joan and Frenchie and Kate and Hungarian Joe have been dancing. Joan pauses, looks around the room. "Where is Shannon?"

Frenchie says, "I saw her and Jacques go outside."

Joan says, "I've got to find her. I told mother I would watch out for her." She goes to the coat rod and grabs her coat and Shannon's. Frenchie helps her put her coat on. They go out the front door and into the farmyard.

Frenchie says, "That's Jacques car over there." He points to a 1935 Ford. They approach the car, bang on the steamed-up window. Inside, Shannon knows she's been caught. Skirt up, half undressed, she adjusts her clothes. She and Jacques get out of the car.

Joan says, "I didn't notice you left the party." She looks Shannon up and down and hands her the coat she carried over her arm. Shannon blushes, says, "We were right here." Joan says, "We better get you home before you get yourself in trouble. Shannon reluctantly pulls herself away from Jacques. He gives her a kiss on the cheek, blows in her ear. Shannon twitches with delight, still open, expectant.

Chapter 3

It is springtime. The lilacs are in bloom. Jacques is sitting at kitchen table with two middle age people, a man and a woman, his parents, Catherine and Joseph.   Catherine is tall for a woman, 5'10", with large bones and strong arms. She dresses in flowered house dresses, wears black oxford shoes, and works like a horse. Joseph is fat, carries a paunch from good food and good wine. He is strong as a horse. He grows the food and makes the wine. Catherine cooks.

These people are farmers, but not just any farmers. Their farm is a whole section of land, that is 640 acres. Their farm is one of seven that stretch the full length of the road. The farm came from Catherine's side of the family. Each of seven sisters was given a farm with a full section of land. They married seven brothers, all farmers. The father who passed out the farms to his daughters was seven foot tall. That's where Catherine got her height.

Joseph is probably the best farmer among the brothers. His rows are perfectly aligned, never a zig or a zag. He only went to the fourth grade, and was a poor student, so he barely can read and write. But he knows how to farm, how to raise cows and pigs and turkeys, how to butcher, how to make money. He is such a strategist that when the price of soybeans was going down, he built silos to save his beans. Then he sold them for seed at four times the price for soybeans.

Joseph has a slaughterhouse on his property, and he butchers the cows and pigs there. He also has 30,000 turkeys that he grows and sells to the people in Detroit for their Thanksgiving. Turkeys are so dumb that a bolt of lightening or a loud sound will actually scare them to death. Joseph knows they have no way to gauge reality, so he protects them in houses. He married Catherine for the farm.

Catherine turned out to be the best farm wife possible. She never tires, can drive a tractor and run a kitchen. If you bring her a goose or a pheasant, she will clean it, pluck it, cook it, and serve it. She never complains. She always has tins of donuts and cakes and cookies. She cans all summer. If someone drops by, the food comes out from seemingly nowhere and loads up the table. They never "run out" of anything.

Joseph and Catherin are workers. They get up early and work – feed the cows and the pigs and the chickens and the turkeys. Then they have breakfast and go back to work – out in the fields. Then they have lunch, take a nap, and go back to work - back out in the fields. In between, Catherine takes care of the kitchen. Joseph grows his own grapes and makes his own wine. In the spring he gathers the dandelions and makes wine from them. In the summer, he harvests the elderberries alongside the road, and he makes wine from them. He keeps the wine in oak barrels at the bottom of the stairs on the way up to the kitchen. When he comes in from the field at the end of the day, he fills his cup with wine..

On Sunday morning they go into town to the Catholic church on

the corner. There they all are, the seven sisters and the seven brothers.
After church they stand around and talk before they get in their cars
and go home to the big Sunday dinner.

Catherine always prepares the food before she leaves for church,
and she has it on the table in half an hour. On Sunday afternoon the
priest and one or more of the relatives will come over, and they play
cards and drink wine and Canadian Club whiskey.   This is the life of
Catherine and Joseph.

Jacques is the only child of Catherine and Joseph. He is expected to
work the farm, then inherit the farm. Joseph lets him sell the hides
from the cows and the pigs he butchers. Jacques always has money,
more money than any of his friends. Joseph and Catherine sent him to
Assumption College. Joseph wishes he had gone beyond the fourth
grade, that he could read. He expects his son to make up for what he
can't do. There is only one problem. Jacques hates the farm, hates the
farm-work, hates the farm life.

The conversation at the kitchen table is tense. Jacques has married
Shannon, age 15. Shannon is five months pregnant. Jacques wants to
bring her home to the farm. Catherine seldom smiles anyway, but
today she is particularly stern: "There is no room in this house for that
kind of girl. You had to marry her, but you can't bring her here."

Jacques says, "We have nowhere else to go. We can't stay with her
parents in Detroit. The house is too small. They have eight kids. I
dropped out of college. I will work on the farm and in the slaughter

house to pay for our keep."

Joseph looks with pity on his son. He vaguely remembers what it was like when he was young, to want a girl's body. That was a long time ago. He never really wanted Catherine's body. Not that way. He wanted her body to work the farm. He remembers a girl, in the haystack, when he was sixteen and she was seventeen. They took a roll in the hay. She was visiting her aunt and uncle and offered to help in the field. They put her to hoe the field with Joseph. She teased him, and he chased her to the barn. She fell on the hay, smiled up at him, and he fell on top of her. He kissed her. It's the first time he kissed a girl. She touched him before he touched her. She had done it before, knew what she wanted. She guided him, told him where to put it, how to do it. He had never felt so alive.

The next day they did it again. Then she had to go home. He remembers worrying. If she got pregnant, they would come and get him. She would tell. It wasn't worth it, doing that. Catherine doesn't like it. That is fine with him. When you live on a farm and you get bulls to do it to cows, hogs to do it, watch them do it, it's no sacred thing. It's a bestial thing. Not that he considers Jacques bestial.

Catholics have to get married. Jacques is Catholic. The Irish girl, what's her name, she's Catholic. Joseph doesn't know where it happened or how, but this girl enticed his son, and now he is stuck with her because he stuck her. He understands her family, wanting to make it right for her. He understands, too, that they don't have room in their house for two more. What does her father do? Takes a lunch pail to

14

work. Joseph never had a lunch pail. This is not what he wanted for his son, his only son, dropped out of college. But Jacques is accepting responsibility, his responsibility. Joseph respects that.

"The house is Catherine's house, so it is her decision. Your mother is in charge of her house. If she says 'no,' it's no." Joseph looks at Jacques, sitting there at the table, asking them to help him, to let him bring the girl there.

"I'll tell you what I can do. You can have the chicken coop, the one that's empty. We haven't had chickens in that one for a couple of years. You will need to clean it out, especially if you are going to put a baby in there. You'll need a stove to keep the child warm in the winter. I'll buy you one and put it in there."

Chapter 4

Shannon didn't tell her sisters they went all the way. Joan and Kate asked questions on the way home, lots of questions. They were worried that they didn't do what they promised Kelly – take care of Shannon. They were too busy enjoying themselves, getting attention, dancing, taking a sip, but just a sip. They got it out of her that she drank a whole glass of the spiked coke, that Jacques got her drunk. She told them he kissed her, that he touched her, but that was all. They carefully planned their story for Kelly.

Frenchie had really liked Joan. He began driving over to Detroit to take her out. Jacques didn't come. Shannon was ok, but she was too young. He was a "college man" and she was only 15. And she was a little crazy, too much of a handful. Kelly thought it was a good thing they went to the party if Joan got a boyfriend out of it. She felt sad for Kate, and she was relieved about Shannon.

Then Shannon missed a period. She didn't say anything. She hadn't had her period very long, just since she was 13. She had read the book about the flowers and the bees, and she knew at first you might skip. And then she missed again. Who to tell: Her mother, Kelly, would get mad. Her sisters, Joan and Kate, would worry about their own hide because they were irresponsible in looking after the little sister. Shannon decided to tell Mick after he had soaked in gin. If he got upset, he probably wouldn't remember the next day.

Mick was sitting on the front porch on Friday night. It was the end of the work week. He always stopped to cash his check and buy his gin for the week before he came home. Kelly met him at the front door, took the rest of his paycheck money, and booted him out of the house. If she didn't get the money on pay day, she wouldn't get it. Shannon went out on the porch and sat down next to him. She said, "Pa, I need to tell you something." Mick had just enough gin that he was past the spike and was getting sleepy.

Shannon began, describing the whole night, the party, the coke, going to the car with Jacques. When she got there, Mick said, "Don't tell me he did it to you."

Shannon said, "Yes, and now I've missed two periods. I'm afraid to tell Ma."

"Holy Jesus, Mother of Mary! You're going the way of your mother, Kelly Clancy."

Shannon began to cry. Mick put his arm around her, cuddled her head in his neck, and in his drunken stupor said, "I will go get the bastard." The next morning he remembered. He said to Kelly at breakfast, when all of the children cleared out of the kitchen, "Shannon and I need to have a talk with you."

Kelly Clancy recognized the serious tone, sober, not gin-soaked, and sat down at the kitchen table. Shannon wasn't there. Kelly looked

Mick in the eye and said, "Is she knocked up?" Mick said, "Yes." Kelly said, "I noticed she's been acting peculiar, not her usual happy self, busy about everything she's doing. And she's not eating. What are we going to do?"

"He's a friend of that Frenchie that's taking out Joan. Frenchie will have to take me to him in Canada."

That was two months ago, and now here was Shannon, five months pregnant, belly beginning to protrude, standing in the middle of the chicken coop. Mick had hunted Jacques down at Assumption College and told him, in no uncertain terms, that he had to marry his daughter. Jacques took it like a man. He didn't try to lie and get out of it. He knew what he and Shannon had done. He was a Catholic boy. He knew he had to bite the bullet or take the bullet. There nothing quite like the ire of an Irish father.

The next day Jacques drove to Detroit and met with Kelly, Shannon, and Mick. Shannon was shy with him, held her head down, didn't look him in the eye. Jacques said, "We really don't know each other. Is it ok if we get acquainted before we get married?" Kelly said they could see each other for a couple of months, like they were dating, because Shannon hadn't begun to "show."

So Jacques started driving over to Detroit every evening, taking Shannon out for ice cream or to the show, sometimes helping Mick with projects around the house. Everyone was getting used to him, and he seemed to fit into the Irish family. The only problem was, the house was too small for him to move in. Kelly said he would have to find a place for them to live. On a Saturday morning, Jacques and Shannon, accompanied by Kelly and Mick, went down to the Catholic Church a block away, and the Priest married them. Jacques still hadn't told his parents.

That's how Shannon got to the chicken coop. It was one room about 15 feet long and 12 feet wide. Jacques had cleared everything out that was built in for the chickens. He had poured cement over the floor so that they wouldn't be living right on the dirt. A pot-bellied wood-burning stove was in the middle of the room, just as Joseph had promised. A table with a dishpan and pail was in one corner, with a slop bucket next to it. Along the same wall, there was a coal-burning cooking stove with two burners, and next to that an Ice Box.

Across the room was a cupboard for dishes and a bench that could be used for cooking or for changing a baby's diaper. A mattress was on the floor in the farthest corner of the room with a chamber pot next to it. Next to the mattress was a dresser with a mirror. Jacques had mounted a pole on two sticks to make a closet, and he had a curtain hanging around it. Near the pot-bellied stove was a small table with three chairs. Each table and the dresser had kerosene lanterns. Jacques had tried to make it as tidy and convenient as he could. But it was a chicken coop. There was a pump outside the door, and about 20 feet away, an outhouse.

Shannon's house in Detroit was small and simple, but they had running water and electric lights. Shannon had never experienced anything like this. She was a city girl. Here they were in the country, on the farm, in a tiny town where Shannon didn't know anyone. They all spoke French, and Shannon didn't. And on top of that, Jacques' parents hated her for being a bad girl. They said, "She got herself pregnant."

Jacques and Frenchie watched Shannon pucker up and cry. Jacques put his arms around her and said, "This is all I can do now. When the baby comes, they may change their minds. Now they want to punish us." He looked at this fat little pregnant teen-age girl with red hair and green eyes and thought how he had wrecked his life. No, he couldn't go there. He couldn't even imagine what it would be like with a baby. It was too overwhelming. Jacques and Frenchie went outside. They could leave. Shannon couldn't.

Chapter 5

Jacques is working in the field, dressed in his bib overalls and plaid shirt, running the tractor. He sees a 1938 Ford drive up and stop by the side of the road. A man in a business suit gets out of the car and beckons to Jacques. Jacques gets off the tractor and walks across the field to the car. The man shakes Jacques' hand and introduces himself as Willie Schroeder with the Guaranteed Insurance Company.

Willie is one of those fast-talking salesmen types. He gets right down to business, explaining the deal. His company represents a new thing: Insurance. People buy it to protect themselves from something that scares them. If they are afraid they might die, they buy Death Insurance. But the insurance company calls it Life Insurance because people don't want to think about death. If they are afraid they will wreck their car, they buy Car Insurance. If they are afraid their house will burn down, they buy Fire Insurance. The insurance company makes its money by betting it won't happen, and then they won't have to pay.

Jacques is listening. He bites: "So what's in it for me."

Well, Willie says, you are well known around here. Your father owns this big farm and slaughter house. People respect the family. You can help us sell people on the idea of Fire Insurance."

Jacques says, "So you want me to sell insurance."

Willie says, "No. We want you to burn your house down."

Jacques looks a little stunned, but he's curious. They are still living in the chicken coop, and it isn't much of a house. It would be better off burned down. Willie explains that Detroit and Ontario are new markets for them. They need to sell people on the idea. If Jacques sets his house on fire and it burns down, they will put his picture in the newspaper getting paid by the insurance company, proof that it works.

Jacques says, "How much."

"We'll pay you $500 for burning down your house and the picture in the paper. We'll pay you $100 for every fire you set in Detroit on a house where the people have insurance. We tell you where to go. You figure out how to do it. Once the house is burned down, you get paid."

It didn't take Jacques long to make up his mind. Shannon and Vincent were going to Detroit the next week to celebrate Vincent's first birthday with his family. He just started to walk. He said, "How do I know you're for real? How do I know you'll give me the $500?"

Willie pulled out a $100 bill. "This will be your deposit. All you have to do is call me when it's done. Here's my number."

Shannon is excited to be going home to Detroit. She misses her family. And she is so proud of Vincent. She wants to show him off. He is walking and even talking. He looks just like Jacques with brown hair and brown eyes, and everyone says he is handsome. They are going to stay for two weeks, so she packs up enough clothes. She doesn't need to worry about Jacques. His mother still likes to feed him. He and

Frenchie are always busy at night doing things.

She has never been so lonely. The only person in town who ever comes over is Dolly, and they call her the town prostitute. Dolly has a little boy, and he and Vincent sort of play together, the way 12-month-old children play. Dolly can speak English, and she had to get married, too. But her husband left her right away. She envies Shannon for having Jacques. But she feels sorry for her that his folks won't have anything to do with her. Jacques can take Vincent to the farm house, but Shannon isn't welcome.

Jacques puts Shannon and Vincent in the car with the bags Shannon had packed and heads for the Ambassador Bridge. On the way he says, "A guy came by last week and told me about Fire Insurance. It pays you if your house burns down. For $25 I got $500 worth of insurance for a year. Our chicken coop isn't worth more than that." Shannon thinks that is a good idea. She has nothing to do with money. The only money she ever sees is what Jacques gives her to buy food and clothes for Vincent. Jacques' mother sends things home for Vincent, but never anything for her. She can't wait to get home where people speak English and like her. She misses Joan and Kate so much. Frenchie still goes over to take Joan out, but Joan doesn't want to end up like Shannon in McGregor. She has sort of cooled it with him.

Jacques waits for two days after Shannon leaves before he starts the fire. He pours kerosene in the pot-bellied stove so that it explodes. He also tips over two of the kerosene lamps and lights the kerosene.

Then he goes to the farm and climbs on the tractor. Because the chicken coop is off the main road, it will take a while for the fire to be discovered. He makes sure Joseph waves to him when he drives into the field. After a couple of hours, a neighbor boy comes running up to his tractor: "Your house is on fire, your house is on fire."

Jacques calls Willie, and he comes right over with a photographer from the *Windsor Press*. That is the newspaper delivered to McGregor. Willie hands Jacques the check for $500, and the photographer takes the picture. Willie tells him he can keep the $100. It is a deposit for Detroit. Jacques is in business!

The next day, it is all over the town. The newspaper boy goes up and down the street of McGregor yelling, "Read all about it! Read all about It! Butcher Jacques' house burned down. The Insurance Company paid him $500 to rebuild it. "He holds up the paper with the picture on the front page.

The newsboy makes his way down the street, past the general store, the gas station, the newspaper office, the farm supply store, and the bank. The Catholic church is on one corner and the school on the other. People come out of the only restaurant, The Golden Boar, next to the hotel at the end of the street. That is it for McGregor. The whole town knows the story.

This is the *Windsor Press*, and the story is in the headlines. It says the stove must have exploded. No one was home. Thankfully, Jacques' wife and son were visiting her parents in Detroit. Jacques was out with the tractor pulling the plow in the field. The *Detroit Press* picks up the article. Jacques calls Shannon right away. He doesn't want her to learn about the fire from the newspaper.

It does occur to Shannon that Jacques set the fire. She has lived with him now for over a year and picked up on his ways. She knows he always has an angle, always is calculating, always figuring out a way to beat the system. He has to beat the system. It is the only way to get out from under the thumb of his parents. She doesn't care. They are now out of the chicken coop.

Chapter 6

It is late afternoon, and Jacques and Frenchie are under Jacques' truck, banging around. The truck has a sign on the door: JACQUES PASCAL BUTCHER. They have been installing holding units that can't be seen from the outside of the truck. They brush themselves off and go inside to wash their hands.

Shannon follows them out, a little boy, barely walking, clinging to her skirt. She asks Frenchie If he would like to stay to supper. Jacques says, "We don't have time for supper. Save me something." He gives her a kiss on the cheek and says, "See you later. Frenchie and I have a meeting over the Bridge."

Shannon waves good-by and goes inside to feed Vincent his supper. By now Shannon is used to being alone, day and night. She just shrugs her shoulders. Even though she has just had her 17th birthday, she is beginning to feel inside like an old, abandoned woman. Jacques is never home, and he never takes her anywhere. She has no reason to fix herself up or to dress up, and the worse she looks, the less attention Jacques gives her. She has missed two periods, and when she told Jacques, he got angry and slapped her. Her whole life is tied up in Vincent who is walking and talking but hardly a companion. She ladles out stew into two bowls on the table for herself and Vincent.

As the truck pulls out of the yard and starts down the road, Jacques says to Frenchie: "The farm and butcher thing don't cut it. Shannon is having another baby. How did I ever get myself into this." Frenchie has stopped going over to Detroit to see Shannon's sister. He has seen too much of Jacques' misery first-hand to want any part of being tied down with a girl.

As the sound of the truck winds down, Shannon hears a knock on the door. It is Dolly, the only one in town that ever comes over to see her. Dolly says, "I thought I would just stop by." Dolly is wearing a tight-fitting dress, high heels, and heavy make-up, the very opposite of the way Shannon looks, like a farm-wife. She has a two-year old boy, Freddie, with her.

Shannon says, "Come on in. We were just having supper. Have something to eat." By now Vincent and Freddie have gone off to play together. Vincent loves it when Freddie comes over.

Shannon puts a bowl on the table for Dolly. She says, "Jacques went off with Frenchie again, and Vincent and I are all alone. And Dolly I'm pregnant again. I can't believe it. "

Dollie says, "Isn't that what you said happened to your mother? The apple doesn't fall far from the tree." Then she says, "I can't eat anything. I have a job tonight. Would you mind watching Freddie for a couple of hours? Freddie would like to eat, and he's so happy here with Vincent."

Shannon says, "Freddie can stay the night. It keeps Vincent from missing his Daddy."

Dolly is looking around the house. She says, "You must be getting along better with your in-laws if they let you move in here."

Shannon says, "We're one step up from a chicken coop in this tenant house. But the kitchen isn't really any better than the last one – no running water, a coal stove, an ice-box. I still have to pump water, empty the slop bucket, go out to the outhouse in the dark with a kerosene lamp. They still don't talk to me. Sometimes they ask Jacques to bring Vincent over to their house, but I'm not invited. At least we'll have two bedrooms when the new baby comes and my sister is here. I get so lonely, Dolly. You're the only one who ever comes to see me."

Dolly says, " We women need to stick together. Freddie's father never comes around. I'm so glad you don't judge me." Both women are crying.

As the truck heads toward the Ambassador Bridge, Frenchie begins to fill Jacques in on where they are going. He has met some guys from Detroit that want things smuggled back across the Bridge into Canada where they will sell for twice the price. He figures he and Jacques can work for them until they learn the ropes, and then they can do the business themselves. Frenchie is still taking a few classes at Assumption during the day while Jacques works on the farm. They can do this at night.

Jacques waves to the Guard as they enter the Bridge. It's his cousin. He follows Frenchie's directions, and they turn into a back alley. They park outside of a huge warehouse with boarded-up windows. Frenchie knocks at the door, and a peep-hole opens. Frenchie identifies himself, and the door opens.

They walk in, and once they adjust to the full light, look around to see exactly where they are. The warehouse is divided into sections with signs indicating different brands: Booze: Jim Beam, Old Crow, Old Grandad, Early Times, Canadian Club, Black Velvet, Crown Royal, Lord Calvert. Cigarettes: Lucky Strike, Camels, Chesterfield, Old Gold, Pall Mall, Winston, Muriel Cigars. Four men are sitting at a table counting out money. Each one has a glass of whiskey, and they are smoking cigarettes. The one man wearing a suit beckons to Jacques and Frenchie to join them. The other guys are all wearing work clothes, the same as Jacques and Frenchie.

The guy in the suit pours them a drink. He says, "Fellas, meet Frenchie and his buddy, Jacques. They can help us out across the Bridge." They all shake hands. The man in the suit nods to them to sit down. They both take a swig and listen intently while the guy explains how it works. He asks if they got hooked up.

Jacques says they have it all hooked up under the gas tank. He figures they can carry at least 50 cartons of cigarettes. They are ready to try the first run.

The man in the suit obviously is in charge.. He explains the first run. They just take the cigarettes, sell them, and then bring back the money to split it with him. After that, they use their money from the first run to buy the cartons at the wholesale price and then sell on the other side for profit. Each run they pay back 25% of their profit, and then they're allowed to buy more.

Jacques says they'll start with the cigarettes, see how that goes, and then figure out what to do about the booze. They might have to pay off the Guard, but that would come when they start to make money. They shake hands on the deal, and two of the men at the table get up to help them get started. They load the cartons on a dolly, and push it out into the yard. Jacques gets under the truck, and Frenchie passes the goods to load up. Jacques says, "Hey, Frenchie, this is going to work. They are fitting in just right. We're in business!"

Chapter 7

It is butchering day in the slaughter house in the barn. Joseph has been in the business for years, and he has it down to a science. Now that Jacques is full-time with him at the farm, he likes to stand on the sidelines and allow Jacques to orchestrate the production. A violent rain storm is outside the barn. You can hear the rain pouring down on the barn roof and the thunder and lightening. There is a small leak off to the far side, but it isn't center-stage and insignificant. Joseph runs a tight ship. Even this leak isn't allowed. He will repair it as soon as the weather clears.

A clap of thunder introduces the production, and the barn shakes. This part of the barn has a concrete floor, and the sound hits the concrete and bounces back. The light in the barn is in direct contrast to the darkness outside, visible through the windows. The violence of the storm prepares the stage for the violence about to take place inside. There are twenty men in the slaughterhouse, all wearing overhauls, plaid flannel shirts, and thigh-high rubber boots. They are ready to take their places on this stage.

The room is laid out precisely for this event. Nothing can be left to chance. This is a slaughter house, and slaughter is about to begin. The enraged animals must be contained. Even one on the loose is a death threat. These animals have been fattened up on corn for the slaughter.

They weigh 250 -350 pounds. No single man could overpower one of them.

Two pens are located across from each other on the far sides of the room. The sound of the hooves stamping on the concrete is as deafening as the sound of the storm outside. On the right hand side, the imprisoned cattle bang against the sides of the pen, sensing the danger ahead. They have never before been herded together in such close quarters. The hogs are in the pen on the left side of the room. You can hear them stamping and snorting. The concrete floor is shaking from the pounding of the cattle and the hogs. It vibrates with their apprehension.

A wide runway goes down the middle of the floor, moving upward from the center and swerving so that it is attached to each pen. When the doors are opened, the animals will drive down the runway from the pen to the center of the floor, madly, crazily, rushing to their death. We say "lambs to the slaughter," but the force of the weight on the hooves and the velocity of their futile attempt to escape creates a sound you can never forget, like an ominous, giant boulder that moves at a speed incalculable and unstoppable.

There are huge vats of boiling water in the center of the floor. Long wide tables stretch in front of the vats, with hammers and cleavers spread out along the tables. The twenty men in the slaughter house stand ready for Jacques' order to release the first batch from the pens. They have done this before. They know the sounds they will hear from the pounding of the hooves, the screeches and squeals and bawls and brays. Each one recalls the first time, the horror and the excitement. Now they stand ready, like players about to participate in a circus act where the expectation of the drama creates an adrenalin flow that rushes through their bodies and eradicates all emotions other than the desire to kill. The insane asylum is about to begin.

Jacques has Vincent, now age three, beside him on the floor. He picks up Vincent and carries him to a high stool in the corner. From the corner, Vincent will have a view of the whole operation. Jacques tells him to stay put: "I don't want you down on the floor." He looks around the room, assessing the positioning of the men Five men line each side of the runway, across from each other, holding crowbars. The other ten men are lined up, spread out among the tables and the vats.

Jacques walks to the center of the floor, the ring-leader in this circus, and gives the signal to the two men in charge of the cattle-pen door. They open the door and the stampede begins. As the cattle run past, the men hit them on the head. Vincent is excited by the sound of the hooves and the frenzy of attack. He yells, "Hit them. Hit them."

The other ten men go into action on the assembly line. One slits the cow's throat. Two lift the cow and throw it in the vat of boiling water. Two remove the cow and skin it. Two cut open the cow and throw the entrails on the floor. Jacques paces back and forth, supervising the operation. He prods the men on: "Keep it going. Keep it going."

The pile of entrails is growing higher and higher. The stench in the room is overwhelming: the smell of blood, the boiling flesh, the gas from the entrails as they are jerked out of the animals, the wet hides dumped together in the corner. Every sense is absorbed in the carnage – the sounds of violence and agony, the sight of the blows, the smell of each operation, the feel of the weapon in your hand – the crowbar, the cleaver, the knife. How can such an enterprise be so full of exhilaration. Each man feels part of the whole, mechanical operation. Each one is a vital piece, pitting his survival against the survival of the animal.

Suddenly a bolt of lightening breaks through the barn door, pulling it off its hinges. It flashes down on the floor. The lightening hits the pile of entrails. It thrusts the whole pile up in the air and out the door. The rainwater pours into the slaughter house. It's as if the hand of God has struck.

Vincent stands up on his stool, jumps up and down, enthralled by the drama. Jacques rushes over to his stool, shouts: "Don't move. Stay on the stool."

The men all talk at once, overwhelmed by the spectacle.

"What the fuck"

"Can you believe that!"

"We could have gone out the door, too."

Jacques goes to the barn door, beckons two men to help him, and they close the door. He turns to the men, "The boots saved us. We could have been out there with the entrails." He holds a commanding posture, steady, unshaken. He says to the men, "Now get back to work."

The hogs are next. Jacques signals the two men at the door of the pen to open it. The hogs go pounding down the runway, squeal as their throats are slit, as they are dumped into the boiling water. The pile of hides is tall. Joseph still lets Jacques have the hides to sell.

You would never know from his demeanor how much Jacques hates what he has been doing, hates the vulgar cruelty to the animals, hates the whole operation. He is Jacques the Butcher. It's on his truck. This is his servitude to Shannon and the little boy waiting for him on the stool.

Chapter 8

Shannon is pregnant again. Will this never stop? She always thought her mother was crazy having so many kids. At least her father was home at night, helped her, talked to the kids, played with them. She remembers that he was the only one she felt safe telling she was pregnant with Vincent. It was so different, growing up in an Irish Catholic home where everyone talked to each other, even when they were fighting. And they got up at the same time, ate at the same time, went to school at the same time, went to church at the same time. They laughed and they joked, and they played tricks on each other. They all knew about the gin bottles, and they helped hide them.

These French Catholics were different, just over the bridge and a few miles from Detroit. She always felt like an outsider, like they had God and she was God's bad child. She didn't know whether they really felt that way about her or whether she felt that way about herself. Ever since she got there and Jacques' parents wouldn't speak to her, let her into their home, she began to feel as if she was what they said she was. She didn't know who she was any more. She was Jacques' wife, but she wasn't his wife because his parents didn't acknowledge her. And because his parents didn't acknowledge her, the aunts and uncles didn't acknowledge her.

And when they went to church on Sunday, all of Jacques' aunts and uncles would gather together outside the church. She would wait in the truck with the kids while Jacques talked to them. They never waved to her, spoke to her, asked her to join them. The priest was ok. When she went to confession he told her she was saved, to give them time. Vincent was already three. How much time did they need.

And they would come and get Vincent, but they never took Anthony. He was already a year and a half old. He was too small to notice, but Shannon did. She felt special toward Vincent, too, but Anthony was her son. She wanted him to be treated fairly. Jacques took Vincent places. She supposed Anthony was still too little, that he would be too much trouble. Vincent was old for his age, like he was born knowing he was born as a burden. She didn't exactly mean that. As if he was born knowing that he was the reason his mother was so unhappy. He knew she was unhappy. He knew when she cried, and she cried a lot. They were always alone together. Anthony didn't count. He could barely talk.

But Joan was here, and Shannon was ready to go. It was so wonderful to have company, to have someone to talk to. It seemed like the old times she missed so much. Detroit was only across the Bridge, but it seemed so far away. She didn't drive. And they only had the truck. Jacques always had the truck, day and night. She didn't know what he did at night, but he was never home. He said he was buying and selling things. She didn't know what "things." Something told her not to ask what "things." He would get mad, and then he would slap her. Then Vincent would cry.

She said to Joan, "I'm so glad you're here. The baby will come anytime. I can't believe I will have three kids in four years just because you took me to that party."

Joan smiles and winks: "You always said you could take care of yourself." Joan has no idea how miserable Shannon is. She doesn't talk about it. What good would it do. Then no one would want to be around her.

"Well, at least you didn't end up marrying Frenchie. You would be stuck here, too. Frenchie and Jacques go somewhere almost every night, but he never brings around any girls."

Joan asked, "Do you think he's queer?"

"No, he probably sees how much Jacques has on his hands and figures he's well off."

The sound of a truck is heard from outside, and Jacques and Frenchie come through the kitchen door. Jacques hugs Joan and says, "You probably got here just in time.

Joan observes, "She's about ready to pop."

Shannon is at the stove. She says, "Supper is ready. Frenchie, will you stay?"

Frenchie, looking provocatively at Joan, says, "It's tempting. Jacques and I didn't get our deal tonight, so we can spend it with you two. It will be like old times."

Shannon goes to the stove and begins banging around. Jacques is in the corner picking up the boys, and Joan and Frenchie are sitting at the table set for four. Suddenly there's a puddle on the floor under Shannon. She screams, "My water just broke, Jacques. We need to go to the hospital." Shannon kisses the boys and picks up the bag she has all packed. She and Jacques head out the door.

Frenchie and Joan are alone. She says, "It's been four years since that party when Shannon got laid. Why aren't you married?"

Frenchie says, "Just waiting for the right girl, someone who can stand this town."

Joan replies, "There are other places to live. Shannon would much rather be in Detroit."

Frenchie is going through the cupboards. He pulls out a quart bottle. "I knew there would be some of his Dad's wine here." He pours them both a tumbler. "Jacques and I are in business here together. When we've saved enough, we'll both leave." He looks in the corner. The boys are asleep. He nods to Joan, and she goes to the boys, undresses them, and picks them up one at a time and carries them to the bedroom. Joan closes the bedroom door, goes to the stove, fills two plates, and brings them to the table.

Frenchie raises a glass for a toast to old times. The eating and drinking takes on a sensual rhythm, and soon they are feeding each other and nuzzling each other. Frenchie leans over and kisses Joan. She kisses him back. Frenchie draws Joan to him. She takes his hand and leads him to Shannon and Jacques' bedroom. Frenchie says, "It's been a long time. Now it's our turn." Joan lies down on the bed and pulls Frenchie toward her. He begins removing their clothes. They roll on the bed, he enters her, she cries out with unexpected joy. They fall asleep in each other's arms.

They are awakened at dawn by the sound of a truck outside. They hastily jump out of bed and pull on some clothes, attempting to straighten up. Jacques walks in the kitchen door and announces "Another boy! She did it quick. His name is Frank. " He notices Frenchie and Joan's disarray. "Hey, what's been going on? I hope my boys didn't see you."

Frenchie, with a big shit-eating grin says, "I always did like the sister. We were just getting acquainted again." Joan cuddles up to Frenchie.

Chapter 9

Jacques is overflowing with pent-up rage. He is trapped: Trapped by his child-bride who has managed to load him down with three sons in four years. Trapped by the farm and the slaughter house. Trapped by his parents, Catherine and Joseph, whose only vision for him is the life they had always led, tied to the farm, tied to the slaughter house, tied to McGregor, tied to their sisters and brothers, tied to the church and the priest. To them this is life.

They are among the most prosperous people in McGregor. Joseph is by far the best farmer among all of the husbands of the seven sisters who inherited the farms. Catherine is an exemplary farm wife. She not only tends the house, but also works the fields. She can drive a tractor or a plow. No one can match her cooking. Her coconut cake is famous. If anyone walks into the farmhouse, they walk away stuffed, stuffed with Joseph's homemade wine, stuffed with the food Catherine always has in the pantry, stuffed with the sense of hospitality they share with their relatives and the friends. Jacques is not only stuffed. He is stifled, stalled.

And then there is Shannon. She is only 19. She doesn't know anything. She is an all right mother with the kids, but she doesn't know how to do anything else. She might have learned her way around the farm, but Catherine and Joseph still won't acknowledge her, won't let her come to the farmhouse, won't invite her for Christmas. They have nothing to talk about. She is still pretty, but even that has dimmed. When he met her, she was all fixed up, just like her sisters. There was a spark of joy at the Clancy house, of expectation. None of that is with Shannon now. He knows she is trapped, too, but she can immerse herself in taking care of the boys.

The only one he likes is Vincent. The other two cry a lot. Frank is barely out of the crib, and Anthony is barely walking. Vincent can talk. Catherine and Joseph like him. He looks like Jacques. He probably reminds them of when he was little. Catherine never had any more. They have always put all of their energy into Jacques, all of their attention, all of their expectation. And with Vincent, here is a little Jacques they can spoil and bring up right, to love the farm, to love the business, to love everything Jacques hates.

It is a beautiful autumn day. The trees have all turned, and the pheasants are there for the shooting. Frenchie is in Detroit, back on the hot trail of Joan. They don't have a job. Jacques goes in and takes his gun off the rack on the wall and walks out to his truck. Vincent follows him.

Vincent says, "Daddy, Daddy, please let me come."

Jacques replies, "Ok. You can ride on the fender."

Shannon stands by the door. She has Anthony by her feet and Frank on her hip. She has a determined look on her face. "You can't let that boy ride outside the truck. He could fall off."

Jacques says, "Vincent, get in the front seat." Vincent climbs into the truck. The hunting dog jumps in the back of the truck. Jacques can't wait to get out of there, away from Shannon. He takes off with a screech of the tires.

Vincent says, "Whee, this is fun. Go, Daddy, Go."

Jacques reaches through the back window and pulls his shotgun from the back of the truck. He is heading down the main street of McGregor. He puts it on the floor of the front seat. He suddenly has the impulse to just start shooting. It's like he goes into a rage, a rage he can't control. All of the anger that he has been stuffing, the anger at Shannon, the anger at Catherine and Joseph, the anger at the farm, the anger at the stench of the slaughter house, all of it just breaks out of him. He stops the truck in the middle of the street, picks up the gun, points it out of the window and shoots. This is blind rage.

Jacques puts down the gun, drives to the end of the street, and parks. He gets out of the truck and starts shooting at the hotel windows. The people on the street stand by in terror. They hit the ground. Vincent is caught up in the drama of the action. He cries out:

"Bang, Bang, Bang! Shoot, Daddy, shoot."

Jacques gets back in the truck.

He says, "That will show them!" He backs up his truck, turns it around, and heads back down the main street. People on the street watch from the curb, frozen in   place, in total disbelief.

Vincent says, "That was fun, Daddy. Let's do it again."

Jacques drives on through the town and out to an open cornfield. He gets out of the truck and lifts Vincent out of the truck. The dog jumps out of the back. Jacques carries his gun.

Vincent has never hunted before. He follows Jacques and the dog into the cornfield. He can only see the bottom of the stalks. It feels like a jungle to him. It is a bright autumn afternoon, and he can smell the corn stalks warm by the sun. He tramps along the furrow, following the dog. He feels excited, but he doesn't know exactly why. He just knows he is with his Daddy, that they are together, that it's only Jacques and him, and they are having an adventure.

Suddenly the dog stops, points. Jacques stops. The only sound is the sound of wings breaking up through the corn, up into the sky. Jacques watches them in flight overhead, aims carefully, points only toward the cock bird. It is illegal to shoot the hens. The bullet connects, the cock falls to the ground, and the dog runs to pick it up. He drops it at Vincent's feet,

Vincent has never seen anything more beautiful. The feathers of the dying bird are vibrantly colored, rust and red and orange. Vincent touches its body, feels the warmth of the breast. He picks it up by the tail and trudges on behind Jacques who walks ahead, his shotgun raised and cocked.

The dog points again. The same fluster of wings is heard as the birds fly up through the cornfield.   Jacques aims, fires. The cock bird falls. Vincent calls out, "Yea, Daddy, yea." Each time the dog points, Jacques aims, fires again, and again, and again. Each time the bird falls. Vincent can't carry any more.

Jacques says, "That's enough. Let's take these to your grandma."

He takes the pheasants from Vincent, and they trudge out of the cornfield. He throws the pheasants in the back of the truck. The dog jumps in, and Vincent climbs into the front seat. Jacques starts up the truck and turns down the road. He heads up to the farmhouse and honks the horn. Catherine and Joseph come out of the house. Jacques jumps out of the truck, holds up the pheasants for Catherine to see, and says, "We're here for supper."

Chapter 10

It's now early November. Vincent tags along with Jacques whenever he can, no matter what he is doing. On this particular Saturday afternoon in early November, Jacques is pitching hay in the barn. Frenchie is back in Detroit again. Vincent has his own little broom, and he is sweeping up after Jacques, organizing his little pile of hay for Jacques to pitch back up. The barn door is open. Next to the barn, you can hear the pigs snorting in the pig sty. Two giant hogs are wallowing in the mud. Vincent runs out every few minutes to toss something to the pigs. He loves to watch them chase and catch and gobble up.

Vincent looks down the road and sees a car approaching. He cries out, "Daddy, Daddy, someone is coming."

Jacques continues his pitching. The car stops by the barn door, and two very tall and heavy black men in suits get out of the car and come to the barn door. They see Vincent and say, "Hey Kid, we're looking for Jacques."

Vincent says, "That's my Daddy. He's in the barn." He says, "Daddy, Daddy, some men are here."

Jacques comes out of the barn, holding his pitchfork, and stands by the pig sty. He says, "I'm Jacques. What can I do for you."

One man is older than the other and takes charge of the conversation. He says, "We have some buddies in Detroit who asked us to look you up."

Jacques shakes both of their hands, and then he says, "You came on a great day. Vincent, you stay here in the barn. I want to show them something."

He beckons them to come over by the pig sty. The two men stare down in the sty and see the two giant hogs rolling around in the mud. They're from the city, and not used to looking at pigs. The youngest man says, "How much do they weigh."

Jacques says, "About 300 pounds. It's almost time for us to butcher them."

Then, taking the youngest by the arm, Jacques says, "Here's something special for you. " He points at a path that runs alongside the barn all the way to the end. "That' s our hog run. Walk on down to the end. There's another sty down there with a sow. She has a litter of piglets."

The young man walks on down the hog run. Jacques turns to the older man standing by the sty, mesmerized by the sight and sound of the hogs. He says, "Did the fellows in Detroit have a message for me?"

The guy says, "Yes, it's pretty straight. They said 'Pay up or else.'"

Jacques is leaning on his pitchfork. He picks up the pitchfork and hits the man on the head. He falls to the ground. Jacques picks him up and throws him in the sty. The hogs begin to tear him apart.

Jacques waves to the younger man standing and watching the sow and the piglets. He yells, "You better come here. Your friend just keeled over. I think he may have had a heart attack."

The younger man comes running down the hog run. When he gets to where Jacques is, Jacques hits him over the head with the pitchfork. He falls to the ground. Jacques picks him up and throws him into the sty. The hogs are having a feast day.

Vincent is standing by the barn door, observing all of this. He says, "Daddy, why did you do this?"

Jacques says, "They were bad men. They came to hurt me." He goes to their car parked by the barn. The keys are in the ignition. He says to Vincent, "Get in. We're going to take a ride." He drives down the road about a mile and turns toward the bridge. He pulls over and parks the car beside the road. He gets out and lifts the hood, so anyone can see that the car had trouble. He says to Vincent, "You can get out. We'll leave the car here. We're taking a walk."

Jacques takes Vincent by the hand, and they head into the woods beside the road. It's a shortcut back to the barn, and no one saw him park the car. The coast is clear. Jacques is relieved it was so easy. He and Frenchie have been way behind in their payments at the warehouse, and he had been expecting a "collection call." It couldn't have been more convenient for it to happen just when he was pitching hay in the barn beside the sty. If he had tried, he couldn't have planned it better.

When they get back to the barn, Jacques closes the door. He says to Vincent, "That's enough for today. Let's go do a little hunting." They climb in the truck with the sign JACQUES PASCAL BUTCHER, and Jacques heads for the cornfield. He says to Vincent, "This is our secret. Don't tell anyone about feeding the pigs." Vincent is already tuned into the next adventure. Jacques makes sure to wave to a neighbor as they turn off the road. He even takes two of the pheasants home to Shannon. He hands them to her and says, "Vincent and I went hunting this afternoon."

The next morning right after breakfast, Jacques goes out the back door to his truck. Vincent hangs on, "Daddy, I want to come."

"Not this time, " Jacques says. Jacques has the bones in the pig sty on his mind. He can't imagine that anyone would come looking for the two men at his farm. No one came down the road when the car was parked by the barn. He made sure that he stopped to tell Joseph and Catherine they were going hunting, and he stopped and chatted with a neighbor on the way. But just to be sure, he has an idea what to do. It's Sunday morning, and everyone will be at church.

He climbs in his truck and heads down the road, back to the barn . He pulls up by the pig sty and opens the gate to the sty. He calls, "Sui, sui, sui." The two hogs pull themselves up and out of the sty. He drives the two hogs down to the other end of the hog run and locks them behind the gate.

Jacques opens the barn door and goes in. He comes out with a big fishing net and a large bucket. The tractor is in the field about fifty yards from the sty. Jacques goes to the tractor, gets on, and drives it up to the barn. He picks up the fishing net and starts fishing bones out of the sty. He empties the net into the big bucket. Each time the bucket is full, he gets on the tractor and drives out into the middle of the empty field. Joseph has just completed the harvest and the field won't be planted until spring.

Jacques gets off the tractor and empties the bucket full of bones, scattering the bones on the fallow land. Then he gets back on the tractor and runs over the bones, again and again, until they are shattered to smithereens. Now he has a rhythm going. He drives the tractor back to the sty, fishes until he has a bucket full, and then drives back out to the middle of the field. It takes him ten trips. "Damn, those bastards were big!"

Chapter 11

It's the last Friday in the Month. Jacques is on his way to his friend's house in McGregor, where they all gather once a month. He and Frenchie have a deal. Every other Saturday, Frenchie will go into Detroit to see Joan. And the last Friday of every month, he will have off. It gives them both a break. The business with Frenchie is going ok, but they had a breakdown with the Warehouse in Detroit. The Warehouse was cheating them, so they stopped paying. They have a new source that is working better, but that's why the Warehouse sent the black guys to get him.

So far, Jacques hasn't heard anything about the black guys. He has stayed away from the place where he parked the car. He didn't want to go near it. It has been two weeks. He heard Vincent tell Shannon that he helped Daddy feed the pigs before they went hunting, but that was all.

Vincent is a pretty smart little kid. He knows where his bread is buttered when it comes to Jacques. If he wants to go with Daddy, he has to do what Daddy tells him. Jacques doesn't mind taking him along. He rather enjoys it. Vincent always throws himself into whatever they are doing. It helps that he looks just like Jacques. Catherine and Joseph adore him, can't get enough of him. But they still will not speak to Shannon. It has been four years now.

Jacques can't help but go back again and again to the trap he is in.

Only 24, saddled with three kids, tied to the farm and the slaughter house. The only "fun" he has is shooting his gun, whether through a window or killing a pheasant. It gives him an outlet for his rage. That rage wells up inside him so bad that he feels as if he would burst or break.

He likes the excitement of his business with Frenchie, and it keeps him away from home. The truth is, home with Shannon is hell. He really has lost all interest in her. He doesn't think Anthony and Frank are his. He brought Shannon to this Friday night party twice. And twice she got pregnant right after. He avoids looking around town to see who the boys might look like. Frank actually looks Irish like a Clancy. But Anthony? No way. He never says anything to Shannon, but it makes him not want to touch her, not to be around her, not to be with the boys, just to stay away. That's why he likes taking Vincent and going away somewhere.

Will he turn out like Joseph with Catherine? But Catherine works in the fields. She and Joseph like the same things. They grew up together. Seven girls from the same father's farm married seven brothers. Joseph picked Catherine because she is so strong and loves to work. She doesn't begrudge Joseph the farm her father gave him because Joseph is such a good farmer. Catherine and Joseph were meant to be together. Catherine doesn't care about sex, doesn't like sex. She doesn't mind when Joseph touches the breasts of young girls at church banquets.

They always say "Here comes Uncle Joseph." And they laugh. And

Catherine comes up behind him and kicks him in the ass with her black oxford. Catherine actually encourages Joseph, in a way eggs him on, because it keeps the sex drive away from her. They live around so many animals that Catherine just thinks it is all disgusting. At least they did it a few times to get Jacques.

Jacques and Shannon have nothing in common except one night of drunken sex. Jacques hates the priest, hates the Catholic church, hates the fact that he "had to get married" to a "girl who got herself pregnant." He can never be a farmer, and Shannon can never be a farm wife. So now what. What next? How can he get out of it. He can't feed Shannon to the pigs, at least never very easily. And then he would be stuck with three kids, maybe only one of them his.

Jacques parks his truck in front of his friend's house. Most everyone else walked there because they live in town. McGregor isn't very big. The guys all have jobs at the general store, the hotel, the newspaper, the Golden Boar. There isn't anything to do in McGregor, not even a movie. Jacques has to go to Detroit to see a movie. When he goes to Detroit, it is for business. When he goes to Detroit, he is with Frenchie. The only time he takes Shannon to Detroit is to leave her off to visit the Clancy family. Shannon wishes she could go back. Jacques guesses Shannon is as trapped as he is.

Jacques knocks on the front door, and his friend opens it. There are about twenty people in the living room. They are all standing around, having a few drinks, laughing, telling jokes, having a party. But it isn't the kind of party where he met Shannon. That seems so long ago, that night at the farmhouse with his College buddies. He doesn't see any of them any more except Frenchie and Hungarian Joe. They all finished school and moved away, some to Toronto and some to Detroit. Jacques is the only one who got caught.

Shannon was the prettiest girl at the party that night. When he put just a little rum in her coca cola, she totally lost it. He had complete control over her. She had no idea what she was doing. But she was hot, eager, there on the make, there to be made. She isn't hot anymore. She has gained weight. Her hair is a mess. She never makes herself up unless she is going to Detroit.

Everyone greets Jacques when he comes through the door. He is the reason they are all there. He is the reason they get together the last Friday of every month. Jacques doesn't think of himself as a leader when he is working at the farm, except when they are slaughtering. Then he is in control. When he comes to these gatherings, these parties, he is a leader, too.

"Ok everyone. Pour yourselves another drink. "

They all fill up their glasses and then sit down on the floor around the low table in the middle of the room. The women are giggling. They are all dressed up for the night, with heavy make-up and some in low-cut dresses. None are older than 30. Most have small children. This is their chance to get out of the house, to have a little wicked and reckless fun. Dolly and Jacques are the only ones there without a mate. It balances things out. Jacques brought Shannon twice before. Both times she got pregnant. He has had enough of that.

Jacques says, 'Ok fellas, throw your house keys on the table."
Jacques doesn't throw in his house keys. He uses his truck keys because
his friend lets him use his house.

"These are the rules. The women will be blindfolded by their
husbands and will, one at a time, pick up a set of keys on the table.
When all of the keys are taken, the blindfolds will come off, and each
woman will know whose keys she has. She will go home with the owner
of the keys, to do whatever they decide to do. Rule #1: Men, use a
rubber. We don't want any accidents. I think I may have accidents
already from bringing Shannon here. Go and enjoy yourselves. When
you are through, at 11:00 p.m. , you will all return to your own houses."

Each man blindfolds his wife. Jacques blindfolds Dolly.

Chapter 12

Shannon is in the kitchen chopping vegetables to put in the stew. Jacques is supposed to be home for supper. He is hardly ever there for supper, but when he is, he likes stew. One thing she always has, plenty of beef and pork. Meat is so expensive in Detroit that it is rationed at the Clancy house. When Jacques first found out Shannon was pregnant, he used to bring meat to her house. Her parents loved him for that. Her parents don't exactly love him anymore. They seldom see him except when he drops off Shannon and the kids for a visit and then comes back to pick her up.

Shannon cuts the beef roast into squares and drops it into the pot to sear. She likes the hiss of the meat searing. How dumb is that. But there are so many things Shannon doesn't like, that it is fun to do something she does like. Once the meat is seared, she adds the vegetables to the pot and tosses in a couple of cups of water. She will let it simmer until Jacques comes home.

A knock is heard at the door. Shannon opens it, and there is Dolly with little Freddie. Dolly says, "We just stopped by for a visit."

Shannon says, "I'm always happy to have company. Boys, take Freddie outside to play so Dolly and I can talk."

Vincent and Anthony head for the door with Freddie. Frank is too small. He sits in his high chair.

Shannon says, "I'll make some tea," and she goes to the sink to fill the tea kettle, puts it on the stove, and takes down a teapot and measures out tea. Dolly sits down at the kitchen table.

Dolly says, "I've got something to tell you that you won't want to hear."

Shannon replies, "Is it about Jacques? He gets meaner and meaner. It doesn't matter what I say. It makes him mad. Then he hits me."

The tea kettle whistles, and Shannon pours the boiling water into the teapot. She brings it to the table and then goes to the cupboard to take out two cups. She pours out the tea.

Dolly says, "He's been playing the Mating Game at least one night a month. You know what that is all about. He brought you a couple of times. I didn't want to mention it to you. You've got enough on your hands. But now, one of the women is pregnant, and she claims Jacques is the father. I don't know if she can prove it, but she has picked Jacques' key quite a few times."

Shannon is filled with revulsion. She remembers her own experience with that game, with the men she was with. Jacques thought it was so much fun. He seemed to like doing that with other women more than he liked doing it with her. For her, it was a chance to get out of the house, to be with other people, to be with another man. After they were there, then Jacques seemed to be more interested in her, as though the whole thing aroused him. And then both times, she got pregnant, first with Anthony and then Frank. She was pretty sure both boys were Jacques', but how could she tell. Both times she had been with different men in town. They were supposed to wear a rubber. She didn't even know who they were.

Then Jacques announced that they weren't going to play that game anymore. She had no idea he was still at it. But then, how would she know. He was never home. He could be anywhere. Shannon felt like she could confide in Dolly. Dolly was always there at the game. Sex for Dolly was a way of life. It was how she made a living for her and Freddie. But she liked it, too. Shannon assumed that's why she played the game. She never really asked her about it. Shannon didn't really know how to talk about sex. She just knew Dolly was the only friend she had.

Shannon says, "What can I do about it? I am here alone. His parents still don't want anything to do with me. They like Vincent, but they never take Anthony or Frank to their house. I don't have any money, and Jacques barely gives me enough for food, except what he brings from the farm. You are the only friend I have. Your reputation around town doesn't matter to me. Jacques resents that I talk to you."

Dolly replies, "I didn't know if I should tell you. The other woman told her husband. It may get out of hand. I thought you should be warned."

Shannon replies, " I will discuss it with the priest. He knows about the game. I took it to Confession. He knows how unhappy I am."

The boys burst in the door. Freddie and Vincent have been fighting over a ball. They want the mothers to solve the problem. Vincent says, "Freddie hit me."

Freddie says, "You hit me first, Vincent."

Dolly says, " Come on, Freddie, it's time to go." She and Freddie start out the back door just as Jacques' truck pulls up outside the house. Vincent and Anthony run out of the house to greet him.

Jacques walks into the kitchen and says, sullenly, "What was that woman doing here?"

Shannon replies, "She just stopped by for a cup of tea. She's the only friend I have."

Jacques says, "I don't want you to talk to her. She's an outrage. No one respects her. "

Shannon says, "She has to earn a living. Freddie's father never gives her a penny. He never comes to see Freddie." Shannon pulls herself up for a fight. "What do you know about respect? Dolly says that you've been playing the Mating Game. You didn't tell me. You told me that was over for us. She says you have been going every month. She knows because she is always there. And she says now one of the women in town is pregnant with your child. Is that true?"

Jacques slaps Shannon across the face and knocks her down to the floor. The rage overtakes him. Who is this awful woman? How can he get rid of her? How can he get away? He grabs the 12 gauge shotgun from the wall and shoves it into her mouth. He stomps her feet. He hears a breaking sound.

Vincent and Anthony are cowering in the corner. They begin to cry. Frank is sitting in his high chair, and he joins in. By now Shannon is hysterical, filled with the pain in her feet and the fear in her heart. How did she ever get saddled with such a monster? She has no one to protect her.

Vincent runs up to pull Jacques away from Shannon. Hatred for his father whelms up in him. This is not the man who takes him hunting for pheasants. This is the man who shoots holes through windows and feeds men to the pigs. His mother takes care of him, feeds him, protects him.

Vincent screams at his father: "I am going to kill you." Jacques shoves Vincent aside, storms out the door. His truck starts up and he's gone.

Chapter 13

Shannon is sitting in the front pew of the McGregor Catholic
Church. Dolly is watching the boys so that she can come and speak to
the priest. Her feet are bandaged, and she has cuts and bruises on her
face and head. Both eyes are black. She has never felt so alone and so
scared. Jacques didn't come home again last night. She is in total fear
of him, not just for herself but also for the boys. She has told the priest
about Jacques' fits of rage. Last night was the worst one she has ever
witnessed. She doesn't know where to go or what to do.

Father John needs more than prayer to comfort her. He feels he
has to act. He has known Joseph and Catherine for many years. They
are among the most faithful and generous people in McGregor except
where this girl, Shannon, is concerned. For her their hearts are frozen.

Father John baptized Jacques. He has known him all of his life,
watched him grow up. Jacques was one of the most promising boys in
town, child of prosperous farmers, going to College, smart, handsome,
eager to learn new things, to experiment. Then he brought this child
bride back to town, a pregnant girl of 15. He has baptized all of the
boys, Vincent, Anthony, and Frank. He hears Shannon' s confession.
Jacques never comes to confession, hardly ever comes to church, works
the farm and has another business on the side.

Jacques is an angry man. Father John has compassion for both of them. It tests his faith. How does God let young people get themselves in these situations. This little girl with three boys never had a chance to grow up. She doesn't have any idea who she is, just what she's supposed to do. Jacques looks at her, at his situation, as a yoke. He always wanted to get away from the farm. That's why he was going to college. And then he had to drop out of school to take care of this family that he didn't want and to live with this young woman he didn't even like.

Father John tried once to talk to Catherine and Joseph about Shannon and the boys, one Sunday when he went there for dinner and cards. Good people can have bad spots, and this was Catherine and Joseph's "bad" spot. There was no Christian charity, no forgiveness, no willingness to allow the little family into their home and into their life. They liked the oldest boy because he looked and acted just like Jacques, but that was the end of it.

He looks at this young woman, barely 20, beaten and bruised. She is crying. Father John says, "When did he do this to you?"

Shannon says, "Last night. In front of the boys. Vincent says he is he going to kill him."

Father John says, "You can't stay here. You need to get out of this town. I'm going to contact your family in Detroit. He has done this once. He'll do it again. You are not safe."

It's a dismal gray day in Detroit, a Saturday morning. Kelly Clancy is sitting at the kitchen table drinking coffee, her hair in curlers, in her favorite chenille housecoat. Mick brought his pay home last night and then tied one on. He hasn't gone anywhere this morning. There is a phone on the wall, the kind you crank up to talk. They have a party line. Whenever anyone gets a call, everyone listens. Kelly gets up to answer the phone. Mick hears the phone and comes into the kitchen. He stands there, listening to Kelly's end of the conversation.

She says, "We had no idea. When Joan was there for the new baby, he was fine. Who is taking care of my daughter?" She listens attentively.

"We've met Dolly. Does Frenchie know?"

Mick says, "Who is it?" Kelly puts her hand over the mouthpiece and replies, "Father John from McGregor."

Mick lets her talk and sits down at the kitchen table. He hears Kelly say, "Since you're sure she needs to leave, I will come and get her. Do you think Jacques will object to having the boys taken away?"

Kelly listens. Then she says, "If that's your advice, we'll prepare to take her by force. I will plan it. Thank you so much Father John. I will discuss it with Mick. Please tell Shannon that you have spoken to us."

Kelly hangs up the phone, goes to the stove, and pours a cup of coffee for Mick. She is crying. "That was Father John from McGregor. He says that Jacques has beat up Shannon, threatened her with a gun, and stomped on and broken her feet. "

Mick says, "That lousy son-of-a-bitch. I'll kill him."

Kelly replies, "First we have to rescue Shannon   Father John says that Shannon and the boys need to escape, that they can't stay there. He says that it's a hostile place for her. Jacques is cruel, his parents are cruel, and she has only one friend, Dolly the prostitute."

Mick says, "What about Frenchie? He's been over here to see Joan."

Father John says Frenchie can't help her. He's in some kind of business with Jacques. Something they do at night. He won't be able to take sides."

"And his parents?"

"Father John says Shannon asked them to help her buy food, and they refused. They won't even talk to her. She has no one on her side who can do anything. It's got to be us. We'll just have to double up and make room for them. I'll get things organized."

Kelly has always known in her heart that it was not going to work, that marriage for her youngest daughter. It seems too familiar, the pregnancy, the shotgun wedding and children one right after another. She did that herself. But Mick is Irish. Like all Irish, he likes to take a nip. If that is the only bad thing, she can live with it. But he goes to work every day at the Ford Motor company, built this little white house, brings his pay check home every week, is someone she can always talk to, is good for a laugh. He is what her father called, "A good, God fearin' man."

Jacques was kind to Shannon just before they were married. He was actually fun to have around. He was cheerful, cracking jokes, teasing the girls. He came to the house, spent time with the family, helped Mick with projects around the house. And he seemed all right after Vincent was born. But the next one, coming so soon, bothered him. And then the next one.

Shannon has mentioned that he is never home, and when he is, he doesn't talk to her. The girls told her. That's how Kelly knows. Shannon hasn't complained. She has accepted that she had made her bed and needs to sleep in it. She begs the girls to come visit, but there is nothing to do in McGregor. Joan says she likes Frenchie, but there is no future. She was not going to get stuck in McGregor. Now Shannon needs to escape from McGregor.

Chapter 14

It doesn't take Kelly Clancy long to get mobilized. She received the call from Father John on Saturday morning, and her plan is to go and bring Shannon home to Detroit the next day. She calls the three biggest Irish mugs she knows in Detroit and asks if they can help her the next day. Fortunately it is a Sunday, and none of them has to work. No one can turn down Kelly Clancy. She is the nicest woman in town.

Kelly goes to the garage and takes down the axe with the long handle. She wraps it first with heavy paper and then on the outside with gift wrap. She doesn't know if she can get it through Customs, and she doesn't know if she will need it, but she is prepared. She starts going from closet to closet, taking out empty suitcases. She packs two into the trunk of the car and puts two on the porch to load on Sunday. She is not going to call Shannon in case Jacques is there. She wants this to be a complete Irish surprise

All three of the men show up at her door at 7:00 a.m. on Sunday morning. Kelly decides they will need two cars, especially since they will be bringing back Shannon and the boys and as much as they can carry. She loads the axe into her 1940 DeSoto, putting it on the floor in the back seat. One of the Irish mugs is sitting in the passenger seat beside her. The other two follow in one of their cars, a 1938 Plymouth.

The two cars head toward the Ambassador Bridge, Kelly in the lead. This isn't the same 1936 DeSoto that carried Shannon to her fateful night just five years ago. Mick insists that they get a new car every two years, so this is the second Clancy car since the three Clancy girls drove over the Bridge to the farm. Mick works at Ford, but likes DeSotos. All three of the mugs are over six feet tall. They tower over Kelly, barely five foot tall and 130 pounds of steel. You can hardly see her head over the steering wheel.

The DeSoto is in the lead. Kelly pulls up to the Guard Gate at the far end of the Bridge. She rolls down the window, and the Customs Officer asks, "Do you have anything to declare."

Kelly says, "Top of the Morning, Officer. We are on the way to visit my daughter, son-in-law and three grandsons. Today is my son-in-law's birthday." Kelly opens the driver's door , gets out and opens the door to the back seat. "The only thing I have to declare is his birthday present. I brought him a fishing pole."

The Custom's Officer says, "May I see it?"

Kelly says, "Sure, and she lifts the long package out of the back seat. "I wrapped it already. I wasn't thinking about Customs. Do you want me to unwrap it?"

The Customs officer says, "That's all right Ma'am. No need to unwrap the present. You go ahead and have a nice visit with your family."

Kelly puts the package back on the floor of the back seat, closes the back door, and gets back on the driver's side. She says, "Thank you,

Officer. That way it will be a surprise for my son-in-law."

Kelly rolls up the window, turns on the car, and slowly pulls away, giving time for the car behind her to get through Customs. She turns to the man beside her, "Well, would you be see'n that! That was close. Thanks be to God he let us through. 'Twas the paper and the bow." They both have a good chuckle.

"You're a clever woman, Kelly Clancy."

She replies, "God is on our side. Let's not forget it."

The cars proceed down a narrow road, past the sign 'WELCOME TO McGREGOR: POPULATION 1505." They pass down the main street, past the hotel, gas station, general store, bank, school. The few people on the street at 8:00 o'clock in the morning stop and stare. They don't recognize the two cars. One of them waves, and Kelly waves back. She pulls up in front of the Church. She goes in alone. The three mugs wait in the cars.

Father John walks up the aisle to greet Kelly, shakes her hand. She told him she would be there at 8:00 o'clock, and here she is. He says, "Good day, Mrs. Clancy. You got here in short order."

"Is she at home?" Kelly asks.

Father John replies, "I called her this morning, just to check. He was there, too. Answered the phone, acting like nothing had ever happened."

Kelly asks, "Does she know I'm coming?"

"No. I didn't want to raise any suspicion with Jacques. I did tell Dolly to be on watch for you. She's very relieved to know you are taking Shannon and the boys. She fears for their lives."

"We'll be on our way then. Please give me a blessing, Father John."

They both do a sign of the cross. Father John says his blessing, and Kelly moves toward the door of the church. "Pray for us, Father John."

He replies, "May you go not in peace, Kelly Clancy. Do the task that must be done. May the Devil be slain."

Kelly gets back in the DeSoto, and the two cars proceed to the front of the tenant house. Kelly and the three mugs get out of the cars, and one mug hands her the package. She unwraps it to reveal the big axe. She walks straight up to the front door and begins to hack through it with the axe. The mug who handed her the axe comes along side to help her. The door breaks apart, and the mugs shove it open.

Shannon and the boys are huddled on the other side, frightened and astonished to see Kelly Clancy come through the door. She sees Jacques by the sink and heads toward him with the axe. He jumps up on the sink and goes out the window.

Kelly says, "Shannon, pack up. You and the boys are leavin' here with us. This place is not safe for you." The mugs carry in the empty suitcases Kelly packed in the cars.

The three boys cower in the corner. Shannon goes to the closet and starts dumping thing in the suitcases. Kelly and the mugs are helping her. They open all the drawers and throw things in. They toss in pictures, toys, a few things from the kitchen cupboard. Dolly and Freddie enter through the axe-opened front door. She warns them, "Jacques has gone to get his friends. He's recruiting help in McGregor. He plans to stop you at the Bridge. You better take the Tunnel."

The three mugs carry the suitcases out to the cars. Dolly hugs Shannon, kisses the boys "good bye." Shannon gets into the DeSoto with Kelly and the mug. The boys climb into the back seat of the Plymouth. They start up the cars.

Chapter 15

Two vehicles are speeding out of McGregor – a truck and a car. The truck has JACQUES PASCAL BUTCHER on the side. Jacques is driving his truck, and Frenchie follows in his own car. Both vehicles have two men in the front seat. They pull up to the entrance of the Ambassador Bridge and parallel park to form a barricade. The Customs officer comes out of his booth and approaches the vehicles. Jacques jumps out, and waves to his long-time friend. The Customs officer asks: "What's going on?"

Jacques replies: "There's been a kidnapping. We are here to stop them."

The Customs officer says, "No one's been here for half an hour. You may be in time. Who is it?"

Jacques says, "They kidnapped my three sons. I'm going to stop them." The four men are out of the car. They position themselves in front of the car. Jacques has his hunting rifle.

In the meantime, the DeSoto and Plymouth pull up at the mouth of the Tunnel. Kelly rolls down her window. The Customs officer comes to check the identification of the driver. Kelly hands him her driver's license. He examines it. Kelly volunteers, "Shannon is my daughter. I am taking her and my grandsons to Detroit for a visit. It's Grandpa's

50th birthday, and we are having a big party for him. The boys are in the back of the other car."

The Customs officer hands back the driver's license. He goes to the next car, checks the driver's license, looks in the back seat to see the boys: He hands back the identification and comments, "Good to see families getting together. Have a great visit." The two cars proceed through the Tunnel.

Back at the Ambassador Bridge, Jacques is pacing back and forth. He says to Frenchie: "They should have been here by now."

Frenchie replies, "Maybe they took the Tunnel."

Jacques say, "Damn. We should have covered that. I'll stay here and you go to the Tunnel."

Frenchie gets in his car and drives away fast. He pulls up at the mouth of the Tunnel and jumps out of the car. He goes up to the Customs booth:

"I'm looking for kidnappers. Has anyone been here with three little boys?"

The Customs officer says, "A grandmother and her daughter came through here about half an hour ago. They were on their way to the Grandpa's birthday party. They are in Detroit by now."

Frenchie gets in his car, turns around with a screech, and heads back to the Bridge to tell Jacques they got away.

In the meantime Kelly and Shannon are home and pull into the driveway of the white house. Kelly honks the horn. Mick and Joan and Kate rush out the front door to greet them. Everyone is hugging and crying.

Mick says, "I can't believe how big the boys are."

Joan says, "Come and eat. We've got Sunday dinner ready. " They go inside. The dining room table is all set. You can smell the roast chicken from the kitchen. Joan and Kate hustle around, filling the serving dishes and carrying everything to the table. Shannon and Kelly just sit. They're too exhausted to move. The three Irish mugs join them at the table. Kelly looks around the table, beaming. She asks Mick to give the blessing.

"Heavenly father. We give thanks today that our Shannon has come home, and that she and the boys are safe. We give thanks for our friends who helped to make this happen. We give thanks that Shannon has escaped into the loving arms of her family and that God is helping us protect her. We give thanks for Father John and for Dolly for alerting us to danger. Please look over us as we learn to live together in this little house, and now bless this food which we are hungry to eat."

Kelly sits at the head of the table and carves the two chickens. By now it is late afternoon, and no one has eaten since early morning. Everyone is starved. Kelly makes sure to give Vincent and Anthony each a drumstick. They pass the dishes with mashed potatoes and gravy and green beans and applesauce. The morning took so much out of all of them. They enjoy the happiness of relief.

When dinner is over, Mick says he and the men will clean up while the women figure out the beds. Joan and Mick and Kate, in addition to cooking, spent the day moving things around in the house to make room for four more people. Joan and Kate show Kelly and Shannon what they have done. They have turned Kelly's sewing room into a bedroom. They have a bed for Shannon, another bed for Vincent and Anthony, and a dresser drawer for Frank. They haven't figured out yet what to do about a closet, but Mick thinks he can put one in at the end of the hall. There is only one bathroom for the whole house. For Shannon and the boys this is a big step up into civilization from the outhouse. Joan suggests they make a morning schedule, with Mick going first because he has to go to work.

The three Irish mugs bring in the suitcases before they leave. There isn't any room in the bedroom, so they leave them in the hall. Shannon will have plenty of time to figure out where to put things later. Shannon and Kelly hug the Irish mugs who have given them the entire day. They laugh and throw the boys up in the air before they leave. They are all just one big Clancy family.

Things quiet down, and Shannon finally has put the boys to bed. As she lies down, she suddenly realizes how completely exhausted she is. There is no going back. This is how it is going to be. Her body aches everywhere from the beating. She thinks about first things first, but everything seems first. She'll have to get a job. Vincent and Anthony will need a school. She will have to get a divorce. How do you do that if you are an American married to a Canadian? What happens to the citizenship of the boys? They were all born in Canada. Is she still an American even though she married a Canadian?

She never wants to see Jacques again. She never ever really did love him. She just went along with the marriage because of Vincent. She had to get married. He has never loved her either. What you do in the back seat of a car has nothing to do with love. Love is more like Mick and Kelly, but they never talk about it. It's what comes with what's convenient becoming such a habit that you can't imagine living any other way.

And you play games with yourself to tolerate the intolerable, like Mick's gin drinking. Not that he's that bad. He brings home his paycheck. And Mick is so kind, so thoughtful, so funny to be around. The boys love Mick. He makes them feel important. Jacques made Vincent feel important, but not Anthony and Frank . He didn't make her feel important. She won't miss him. She might miss Frenchie. Her head aches. Her heart aches. She is so relieved, so relieved, so relieved.

Chapter 16

Time to grow up, Shannon! Wow! That message is coming through loud and clear. She can no longer blame Jacques. She is no longer a little girl. She is 22 years old with three children. She has filed for divorce. Jacques won't contest it, but he won't pay child support. And since she is in the United States and he is in Canada, she has no rights to force anything. He will not have visitation rights because of his record of violence, but his parents will.

They have a roof over their heads, thanks to Mick and Kelly. And they have food to eat, thanks to Mick and Kelly. But Shannon needs to get a job. She needs to start to contribute to the household expenses. Four extra mouths to feed is a burden. Actually it couldn't have been a better time for a woman in Detroit. The war production is booming in the factories, and they are hiring women because the men have all gone to war. Kelly will oversee Vincent and Anthony getting to and from school, and she will watch Frank.

Shannon finally settles on the Ford Motor Company in Willow Run. She can ride the bus to get there and back. The Clancy family still has only one car. She is working the assembly line for B24s, wearing denim coveralls with a polka dot bandana over her hair. She has resumed her provocative display. The coveralls are tight, and she has her voluptuous body back. You would never know she was the mother of three kids.

The whole plant has been converted for the war effort, and

Shannon's job is to drill holes in the fuselage. She and two co-workers, both women, are lined up, side by side. Shannon says, "How long to the break?"

One of them replies, "Fifteen minutes."

"That's good," says Shannon. "I need to call home. The boys had to change schools this morning. The priest kicked them out of St. Andrews Benedict when he found out I'm divorced. I need to check with my mother to see how it went."

The other co-worker pipes in: "That doesn't seem fair, to punish the kids."

Shannon comments, "Stay married. I'm a stamped woman with "Sin" on my forehead. They elected me Rosie the Riveter for one day. Then they found out I'm divorced, and they took it away. Seems like that's all people care about. Priests are the worst. That tumble in the back seat cost me three boys to feed and seven years of sorrow and now shame."

Shannon's call to her mother brings some good news. The priest at St. Henry's says he will take the boys. Kelly told him all about Jacques beating Shannon, the divorce, and the three boys now living with her and Mick in the Clancy home. St. Henry's is not in the Irish neighborhood where they live, and this is not Kelly's priest, but he takes compassion on the situation of the family. It's a bus ride away in the neighborhood with the Eastern Europeans: the Polish , Czech,

Hungarian, Yugoslavian neighborhood. Shannon doesn't care. They can start the next day.

Shannon goes to her supervisor to see if she can change shifts so she can take the boys to school on the bus. The supervisor says, "No," but he does say she can come in two hours late so that she can take the boys to school the first day. So now Shannon has another problem. What will they do after the first day? Shannon calls Kelly back. Kelly agrees to bring Frank and ride the bus with the boys both ways. Shannon could not exist without her parents. When the boys get used to the ride and the school, they will probably be able to go on their own, but not now.

The next morning, Shannon and the schoolboys and Kelly and Frank all get on the bus to ride to St. Henry's. Vincent is turning seven and is supposed to go in the second grade. He's a bright little boy, handsome like his father, and very outspoken. He talks back. It can be a problem, especially with grown-ups who believe a child should be seen and not heard. For all he's been through, he has an air of confidence about him. It might have been developed in McGregor, when Jacques would take him places with him and Catherine and Joseph would spoil him. He's also the first child.

Anthony is different. He doesn't look like either Shannon or Jacques, doesn't seem Irish or French. He is very shy, hangs back, clings to his mother and grandmother. It makes Shannon want to shelter him, to protect him. It started when Jacques didn't take to him like he did to Vincent. Jacques may not be there anymore, but he is still there, in the boys, in the way the boys act, in the way Shannon relates to them. It will always be that way.

They catch the bus the next morning and ride to St. Henry's. It only takes 15 minutes. That's a relief. They go to the priest's office, and he meets the boys. Shannon says, "Father Mark, Vincent is the oldest. He should be in the second grade. Anthony is a year younger. He should be in the first grade."

Father Mark says, "Well, the second grade is full. We do not have any more room. They will both have to go in the first grade."

Vincent says, "Ma, we've been in Polish school for one day, and I have lost a whole year."

Shannon pulls his ear, tells him not to be rude and talk back. They follow the priest to the classroom. He introduces the boys to the nun who teaches the class, Sister Clara. She is elderly the way nuns all seem elderly, with a shiny face and eyeglasses that slide down her nose so she is always pushing them up. You wouldn't guess her age because it wouldn't matter. Nuns don't keep track of such things. Vincent says, " I don't want to be in this class. I want to be in the second grade."

The nun says, "No sassing here, young man. You have a big mouth. You get behind the piano."

Vincent looks around the room, at the other kids, and he defiantly walks to the desk behind the piano. He turns to the room and says, "And don't expect me to play it." He generates a laugh. He's probably on his way to becoming the class clown, or the class troublemaker. At this point Shannon doesn't care. She just needs to get them established, somewhere, somehow.

Shannon and Kelly thank the nun and the priest and prepare to leave. Kelly will meet the boys after school. Kelly catches one bus home with Frank, and Shannon waits for another bus to take her to Willow Run. Shannon has a bag with her coveralls in it. She wore a dress to the school. She will change her clothes in the restroom before she goes on the assembly line. No one at Willow Run has ever seen her in a skirt. As she walks through the gate, two of the guards whistle at her. She appreciates the attention, but has no interest. The last thing she needs in her life right now is a man, any man.

Chapter 17

Jacques continues to live in the tenant house after Shannon and the boys are gone. He doesn't miss them, well maybe Vincent. He had never really cared for Shannon. She was just a pretty girl who got him excited. He drank too much at the party, screwed her in the car, and got stuck with her. Her family wasn't bad. They were kind to him. The whole thing was a huge mistake. He didn't intend to beat her. It's just that the rage would build up in him and he had to let it out.

He knows Vincent is his son. He isn't' sure about Anthony and Frank They played the game enough times that they could be someone else's. And now the neighbor's wife says she is pregnant with his child. How can she prove it.? He got trapped everywhere he turned because he couldn't turn the sex thing off. Shannon is getting a divorce from the U.S. She is gone. He didn't even ask for visitation rights with the boys. They live in Detroit. He lives in McGregor. He doesn't want to live in McGregor.

He and Frenchie have been doing pretty well, buying and selling, and he has some money set aside. Shannon didn't know anything about that. She thought he was just a farmer. If she did, she would probably have asked for it. But it wasn't enough yet to leave. And he is just a farmer. So long as he stays there, he is stuck. He hates the farm. He hates being tied down to the crops. He hates the monotony. He hates being bossed around by Joseph: make the furrows straight. Why is that important?

He is on his way to Sunday dinner with Joseph and Catherine. They are glad Shannon is gone. They want him to come and live with them in the farm house instead of in the tenant house. It is bad enough to be bossed around in the barn, on the tractor, in the slaughter house. He couldn't take it, living with them.

Catherine is such a good cook. She always has pot roast and mashed potatoes on Sunday. He can handle that. He goes in, sits down at the kitchen table, drinks the wine Joseph pours in his glass from the pitcher. There is always wine. Joseph make the best wine. It is in a keg at the bottom of the steps when you come in the door. With Joseph and Catherine there is always more than enough. Except when it came to Shannon. He wondered whether it might have been better with Shannon if they had accepted her, had taken her in, had made her their daughter. But that is all over. He at least is free from that shackle. Joseph is settling in for a long conversation. Jacques dreads it.

Joseph is winding up. "Jacques, you are our only son. Catherine and I do not think much of how you lived with that woman, but now she is gone. We are getting older. We need you to be in business with us. Your uncle, Fez, has offered to sell his farm to us, right next to ours. Your mother and I have decided to buy it and to give it to you. That will give you 400 acres to farm for yourself. If you use the money from the hides from the slaughter house for the farm, you will have enough to buy seed and to hire help."

Catherine has put the food on the table. She comes and sits down. "Now that you're rid of that woman, you can find one who can work and be a proper farm wife instead of a whiner."

Jacques feels the rage rising up in him. He just came for dinner, and now here is a bigger trap. How can he tell them without hurting them. He says, "I don't want a farm wife, or a farm, or a slaughter house. I hate being a butcher and a farmer. You saddle me like an old horse."

Catherine replies, "You are all we got. " She is raising her voice. "You may be stuck with the farm, but we're stuck with you. We need for you to stay here and help us. In a few years, you'll have both farms. You will have hired men working for you. You will be the wealthiest man in town."

Jacques feels his rage getting out of control. He wants to speak the truth, but they don't want to hear the truth. They want him to obey, to be a good boy, to do what they ask, to follow orders. They have never accepted that he might be a grown man. Even when he was married and had a wife and three sons, they never considered him a grown man. Now that the wife and the three sons are gone, he is still not a grown man. What is a grown man? He isn't sure. He has never been out from under their thumb, out from under their rule. And now they want the thumb to be bigger, the rule to be stronger. He knows they won't listen, won't hear him. They only hear what they want to hear. This is their life. They do not know anything else.

Jacques starts to unload: "I hate the farm. I hate farming You can never get away from it, locked in, day after day, week after week, worrying about the weather, and the prices, and the hired help. For me it is like being in prison, with no escape."

Joseph is stunned. They have never had this conversation before. He and Catherine have assumed that what they know is the right way of life, that what they created is good, that Jacques would be grateful, not angry and hostile. He cannot fathom his son's response. They have just given him a 400 acre farm.

Joseph bit his tongue and attempted to be civil: "We all do things we don't like. Even your mother drives a tractor. She goes after the weeds. She takes care of the house and works on the farm. She is proud of what we have accomplished, of what we do. There is goodness in work well done, in being responsible. We stand tall with our brothers and sisters, with the people in McGregor, with the people in church on Sunday. We sit in our family pew, and we are known for our labor and our generosity. This is our way of life. It is your way of life. You are born to it."

Jacques says, "You may be born to it, but I was just born in it. I don't take to it. I don't want it. "

Joseph replies, "We sent you to college, gave you a chance for something else. Then you brought that pregnant girl here and put an end to that. You are back on the farm, and we expect you to stay on the farm."

Jacques stands up, pushes his chair angrily from the table. He face is red with rage. "I don't want your prison. I won't take your prison."

Joseph grabs Jacques by the shoulders and slaps his face. It is the first time Joseph has ever laid a hand on his son.. He and Catherine had vowed when they had a child that they would never hurt the child, never spank the child. Joseph's father had ruled with the rod. They had never wanted to do that. Jacques had always had a free rein, had always been allowed to do and say as he wished. Joseph has had enough.

"Don't ever speak like that again to your mother and me."

Chapter 18

It is Saturday morning, and Shannon is sitting in the kitchen drinking coffee and reading *The Detroit Times*. She is still in her pajamas and housecoat, enjoying her day off from the assembly line. Kelly walks into the kitchen carrying the mail.

There is a letter to Shannon from McGregor. She knows it isn't from Jacques. It's not his handwriting, and he hasn't contacted her since the divorce. She doesn't miss him, doesn't think about him. Her life in Canada is now a nightmare that is over, one she does not wish to relive, even in her sleep. Life with Kelly and Mick isn't perfect, but it works. She is saving money from her job so that she will be able to get a place for herself and the boys. In the meantime she contributes to the household costs from her paycheck each week, and no one complains.

Shannon opens the letter. It is from Jacques' attorney for the divorce, written on behalf of Catherine and Joseph. They do have visitation rights even though Jacques doesn't. She reads it aloud to Kelly: Catherine and Joseph want Vincent to come and visit. They propose to meet her at the Bridge on the Detroit side the next Saturday morning. They will bring him back to the same place at 6:00 p.m. on Sunday.

Kelly asks, "What are you going to do?"

Shannon replies, "They only want Vincent. They never did like the other two boys."

Kelly says, "They had more time to get to know him. He was five when you escaped and came here. Now he's nine. He remembers the farm. The other boys never mention it."

Shannon says, "I'm going to let him go. They have means. They might do something for him."

The next Saturday morning, Shannon puts Vincent in the car and drives to the entrance to the Ambassador Bridge. He has a little suitcase with his pajamas and a change of clothes. When they arrive, Catherine and Joseph are standing by their car at the entrance. Vincent gets out of the car and runs to them. They gather him up in their arms. Shannon doesn't get out of the car, doesn't even wave. She turns her car around and drives away, back home.

She is surprised that she is crying. Just seeing the two of them standing there brought back so many bad memories – the day Jacques took her to the chicken coop, their refusal to give her any money to buy food for the boys, Jacques taking Vincent to visit them, but never the other boys. She wonders how this will affect Vincent. He still says ever so often that he will kill his father. When Shannon agreed to let Vincent visit them, she stipulated to the lawyer that Vincent is not to see Jacques.

She doesn't even know where Jacques is, whether he is still at the farm, whether he and Frenchie have made their escape. She doesn't know and she doesn't care, except she wants to protect her son. He is her boy, but he looks like Jacques. And in some ways, he acts like Jacques, cocky and self- assured and quick to talk back. She can never get the best of him. Sometimes it seems like their roles are reversed, that she is the one taking orders instead of giving them. He is that way at school, too. The nun has complained that he can get the whole class stirred up with just his mouth.

Vincent is excited. He never goes anywhere, and now he is going to Canada. It doesn't seem familiar to him until they start up the road to the farmhouse. They drive past the barn where Vincent saw the lightening take all of the insides of the animals out of the slaughter house, where he watched Jacques feed the men to the pigs. The scene co-mingles feelings of hatred and dread with a strange feeling of coming home. Catherine and Joseph were always kind to him. Catherine fed him her cakes and pies and let him run through the house and out into the farm-yard. He was always happy with them because they made him feel so special. They called themselves Pippi and Mimi, but only to him.

First they go into the house, and Mimi makes Vincent a big bologna sandwich. Pippi makes all of their sausage and bologna and sauerkraut and wine. Mimi makes everything else, even the bread, butter and cheese. It is so good, Vincent asks for another one. Mimi is already busy fixing supper, roast chicken and mashed potatoes and coconut cake. How could he not be having a good time?

As soon as they have eaten lunch, Pippi says, "Let's go outside." He leads Vincent to the tractor and says, "Go ahead. Get into the driver's seat." Vincent climbs up into the seat. It is so far off the ground, it makes him a little dizzy. What if he could drive the tractor? He can just barely reach the pedals. Joseph gets up behind him in the driver's seat, straddles him, and starts up the tractor. He shows Vincent the gears, lets him hold the steering wheel. They drive all around the farmyard. Vincent is squealing with joy and pounding his hands with enthusiasm.

He says, "Let's go faster, Pippi!" He's on top of the world, looking down!

Joseph pulls the tractor up to the barn and turns off the engine. He gets down and lifts Vincent down. He says, "Wait here a minute," and he walks into the barn.

Joseph comes out of the barn carrying a shotgun. Vincent says, "Is that for me, Pippi?"

Joseph says, "Yes. Mimi and I bought it for you. You are old enough now to learn how to shoot."

Joseph and Vincent sit down on a bale of hay. Joseph goes over the parts of the gun, explains how each part works. Vincent listens attentively. Joseph shows him how to take the gun apart, how to clean it. Then Joseph goes into the barn and brings back a box of shells. He shows Vincent how to load the gun. Vincent is a fast learner.

"Ok, Pippi, I'm ready to shoot," says Vincent.

Joseph leads Vincent out to the cornfield where the crows have gathered to eat the kernels left over from the harvest. He lifts the shotgun, aims, and pulls the trigger. A crow falls over. Vincent watches carefully. Pippi lifts the gun again, aims, and pulls the trigger. Another crow falls over.

Vincent says, "Now let me do it." It's a big gun for a little boy, but Vincent raises it to his shoulder, aims, and pulls the trigger. He misses. He says, "I'm going to do it again." He lifts the gun, aims, and pulls the trigger. This time the crow falls over dead. Vincent jumps up and down. "Pippi, this is such fun, the most fun I've ever had."

Joseph says, "The shotgun is yours. You can shoot whenever you come to visit. We will keep it in the barn. Let me show you." He leads Vincent into the barn and hangs the gun in the spot on the wall where it will hang, waiting for his next visit.

Vincent says, "Let's go tell Mimi."

Chapter 19

Vincent doesn't see Jacques when he visits the farm. That is part of the agreement with the lawyer. Jacques has meanwhile yielded to Catherine and Joseph and taken up residence in the home on the adjoining farm. The same Saturday afternoon, he is sitting at the kitchen table with Frenchie and Hungarian Joe. Jacques says, "Let's do double hit tonight. Joe, you go and pick up a load of cigarettes with my truck."

Joe says, "Why do I have to go alone."

Frenchie replies, "We've made a deal with some Chinamen to get them to Detroit. We borrowed a boat. They pay up-front."

A few hours later, while Vincent is asleep in the farmhouse with Joseph and Catherine, Jacques and Frenchie are at the helm of a 30' speed boat with double outboard motors. Frenchie steers. The hold of the boat is filled with cargo in gunny sacks. Jacques comments, "These Chinamen pay a lot better than the cigarettes."

Frenchie replies, "The trick will be getting them up on shore in Detroit without being seen."

Jacques says, "We've got to make this business work. My folks have saddled me down with a farm. They expect me to be a butcher forever. Lucky you never got mixed up with Joan – jut another pain in the ass like her sister." It was not that he could blame Shannon for the

91

farm. Joseph and Catherine saw her leaving as a window to buy him the extra farm. They wouldn't have done that while he was married to Shannon. They didn't want to help him with her. Jacques understood their thinking, had expressed himself. They thought with Shannon gone, they would give him the farm, he would find a better wife, and they would settle down side by side and live happily ever after.

He hates it. He and Frenchie have some money saved from their business, and they took in Hungarian Joe to expand. Jacques figures to make the break, they needed at least $25,000. That would give them enough to move to Montreal, get a place to stay, and invest in some kind of business. There is no way he can borrow on his farm, even though it is in his own name. His uncle is the President of the bank, and he would tell Joseph.

He can't steal from Catherine and Joseph, because they don't put money aside. They have re-invested every penny they earned back into the farm, into seeds, machinery, more cattle, more hogs, more turkeys. More, more, more. They are too young to die. That is an evil thought, but he did have the thought. He thought about setting fire to the house when they were asleep. He knew how to do that.

This Chinaman business might work. They have 20 of them in the gunny sacks, and each one has paid them $100. That is $2000 in one night. Their only cost is renting the boat. When word spreads among the Chinese wanting to get across the border to Detroit, it will bring them more business.

Just then he hears another boat behind them. He tells Frenchie to

92

speed up. Then the other boat speeds up. The Chinamen in the gunny sacks are twitching.

When Jacque looks behind them and sees a Customs patrol boat following them, he asks, "Frenchie, can you go any faster?"

Frenchie says, "I've got it out all the way. This is it."

Jacques says, "These guys will have to go. They're going to catch us if we can't go any faster."

He starts throwing the gunny sacks overboard on the side of the boat away from the approaching patrol. The last one goes overboard just as the patrol overtakes them. The Customs officer jumps on board their boat. He says "What's your cargo?"

Jacques replies, "Nothing officer. No cargo. We're just on our way to Detroit to pick up some friends to go fishing."

The Customs officer looks suspicious. "Why are you in such a hurry?"

Jacques says, "We didn't know who was following us. We thought it might be someone to cause us trouble. It's a comfort to know you are patrolling the river."

The Customs officer says, "I need to look around to be sure you are telling the truth." He moves around the boat, opens doors and looks in, lifts up a mat and sees the storage underneath. He pushes that door open and peers in with his flashlight.

"Where are your fishing poles if you are going fishing?"

Jacques wasn't prepared for that question. He does a double-take, and then , thinking on his feet, says, "Our friends have the poles and the bait. We have the boat. That's how we worked it out."

The Customs officer asks, "Where are you meeting them?
Jacques says, "At the pier at the foot of Woodward."

The customs officer beckons to the patrol boat to come alongside. He says, "Well, then I can be moving on. No need to follow you to the pier."

Frenchie says, "That was too close. You barely got those bags dumped."

Jacques says, "Just keep on going toward Detroit. They may circle back around to check on us."

Frenchie steers straight ahead. They hear the patrol boat moving away, the sound of its motor fading.

Jacques says, "Those Chinamen are probably all at the bottom of the river. I can't imagine how they would get out of the gunny sacks. We got our money. But if word gets out about what we've done, we just killed twenty people."

Frenchie says "We didn't think ahead enough about the patrol boats. They probably have the same officers working every night. So if we start running this boat back and forth, they'll know something's up. That fishing story with no fishing poles can work only once. They'll know we're running cargo."

Jacques says, "Yep, too close. Holy Toledo! That's what they'll say when they wash up on shore down river."

So here is another door closed. It had seemed like a great scheme, the border smuggling business. They had no idea how they would have got the men out of the bags and on to the shore anyway. There probably would have been another boat, a U.S. patrol boat, at the other end. And then they would have been Canadian citizens violating both Canadian and U.S. laws.

Jacques doesn't care about laws or about "the law." He does care about getting caught. Frenchie never has any ideas. He just goes along with whatever scheme Jacques comes up with. But Jacques doesn't want to go it alone. He likes having someone around to talk to. Frenchie and Hungarian Joe are ok guys, as guys go. He accepts defeat for the time being. At least Joe will be back with the cigarettes.

Chapter 20

Vincent has become a regular visitor at the farmhouse in McGregor. Once a month Shannon drives him on Saturday morning to the entrance to the Bridge. Once a month Catherine and Joseph are there to meet him. They always bring him back promptly at 6:00 p.m. on Sunday. For three years he has been using the shotgun Joseph gave him when he made his first visit For three years he has become better and better.

It has never left Vincent's mind that he is going to kill Jacques. He has never forgotten the beating Jacques gave Shannon, has never forgotten their escape with Kelly to Detroit, has never forgotten the promise he made: "I'm going to kill you." For Vincent, learning to shoot gets him ready.

When he goes to McGregor, Vincent never sees Jacques. Catherine and Joseph make sure that doesn't happen, even though Jacques is living on the next farm. Once one of the cousins who came to visit said to him, "Hey, let's go down the road and see Jacques." Vincent said, "Never."

It is a kind of elaborate game of "Let's Pretend" that they are all playing. Shannon pretends that she doesn't resent the fact that Vincent is welcome but Anthony and Frank are not. Joseph and Catherine pretend that they can tolerate Shannon so long as she delivers Vincent to the Bridge. Vincent pretends that he doesn't know that Jacques is down the road waiting to be killed by him when he is ready.

Catherine and Joseph have the picture of a girl with long black hair sitting in the dining room on the sideboard right next to Vincent's picture. Vincent pretends that he doesn't notice the picture of the girl. Catherine and Joseph pretend that Vincent is the only child in their life. Everyone is happier pretending. No harsh words are spoken. No promises are broken. No questions are asked.

Joseph and Catherine have given Vincent a black and tan Gordon Setter to go with the gun. The Gordon Setter is the ultimate hunting dog. It originates from Scotland and got its name from Alexander, the fourth Duke of Gordon, who kept the dogs in his kennels. Gordon Setters are excellent bird hunters because they can easily smell and retrieve the fallen bird. They have tremendous stamina and hunt well on land or in water in all kinds of weather. They are one-man dogs, faithful to their masters.

The dog is a companion at home for Joseph and Catherine, but he waits for Vincent. Vincent has named him Jake, strangely enough, because it sounds so similar to Jacques. That never occurs to Vincent, although he has memories of getting into the truck with Jacques and his dog to go hunting. It was always special for him, and perhaps that lingering memory is behind the great pleasure that Vincent has in just being outside, walking through the picked-over cornfields populated with empty stalks.

It is a late autumn day in McGregor, and there is a light snowfall on the ground. Vincent is now 12. He carries his shotgun down a path lined with colored leaves toward the cornfield. Jake plunges ahead and points. Four pheasants fly up. Vincent shoots. He has learned to take his time, not to shoot too fast and miss because the bullet is in front of the pheasant. One pheasant falls from the sky. Vincent shoots again. A second pheasant falls. Jake goes and brings the first one to Vincent. He pets the dog.

"Good boy! Good boy!

Jake goes and fetches the second bird.

Just then the train whistle blows. The train track runs through the farm. Joseph doesn't mind because sometimes he can ship out his soybean crop by train car. Then the whistle blows again. Vincent watches it go by, and he shudders. He says to Jake:

"You know what, boy. I don't like trains. Never did. They make me sad."

Just then a jack rabbit runs out in front of them. It has a white tail and is almost two feet long. Vincent shoots. This is a Canadian jack rabbit, weighing about 8 pounds of winter weight. Vincent knows the rabbits travel in groups. He waits, standing totally still. Jake is by his side. Another rabbit runs out. Vincent shoots again. Jake goes and gets the rabbits, one at a time, and drops them down by the pheasants.

Vincent can't imagine anything better than this. It's a crisp autumn day, cold but not too cold. He has come to look forward to his weekends at the farm even more because of Jake. Jake stays by his side, waits for his commands, presses against his leg to be petted. At night, when Vincent jumps into the goose-down mattress at least three feet deep on the bed Catherine makes for him, Jake follows. The mattress sinks under their weight, and they snuggle together.

Vincent doesn't have a dog in Detroit. He knows Jake will always be waiting for him, jumping and barking when he gets out of the car, wagging his tale. They are just getting ready to leave the cornfield when a goose flies up. Vincent aims and shoots. The goose falls. Jake retrieves it and drops it on the pile. Vincent says, "Wait until Pippi and Mimi see this. How are we going to get it to the house?"

He gives some thought about how to organize the game. He has a strap with him that he puts around the goose. He then puts the strap over his head so that the goose will be on his back. Then he picks up the rabbits, one at a time. He puts a rabbit on each shoulder. That leaves the two pheasants and his shot gun. The gun has a sling that he can put over his shoulder, under the rabbit on the right. He picks up a pheasant in each hand, and he and Jake start back to the farmhouse.

It's a pretty tough trek, with the weight of all of the game, and Vincent is quite out of breath by the time they reach the porch. He calls out, "Mimi, Pippi, come see." Jake is barking.

Vincent knows they will be in the farmhouse. The harvest is over, and Pippi is in for the winter, drinking wine from his barrels at the bottom of the stairs, eating Mimi's good cooking, and taking naps. Pippi's paunch grows an inch or two every winter, and it is harder and harder for him to get out of his chair.

Catherine comes to the door. She is wearing an apron. She takes one look at Vincent and holds her hands on her hips in astonishment.

She cries out, "Joseph, just come see what this boy has done."

Joseph pulls himself out of his chair and comes to the door. There stands Vincent, two rabbits on his shoulders, a goose down his back, and a pheasant in each hand. He says, "Well, I'll be. Where the hell do you hunt."

Vincent is laughing. He says, "Well, Pippi, the same place you hunt."

Catherine says, "I never saw anything like this before. What a hunter!" She takes the pheasants from Vincent's hands and says, "We're eating pheasant tonight." Then she takes the rabbits off from his shoulders, one at a time, and puts them on the floor of the porch. She says to Vincent, "Today you learn to skin a rabbit." Then she helps him pull the strap over his head to release the goose.

Chapter 21

Joseph wishes Vincent's father down the road would make him as happy as the grandson from Detroit. But he doesn't. It seems like constant confrontation. He drives down the road in early summer, past the fields Jacques has planted. He pulls up to the barn on Jacques' farm and sees Jacques standing by the open barn door. He is leaning on a hay fork. Joseph gets out of his truck. Jacques lifts his hand in greeting and says, "What up?"

Joseph can't hold back his rage: " I just drove past your fields, and the rows are all uneven. I'm ashamed to be related to such a sloppy farmer."

Jacques replies, "You know I don't like this work. Why don't you just hire someone to do it for me. Keep the money from the farm. It's your farm anyway. I don't want it."

Joseph resents his attitude. He and Catherine have given and given to their only son, and this is what they get back. Joseph's rows are always perfect. Everyone in town knows it. They talk about it on Sunday morning after church. He lashes out:

"That isn't the point. A man should take pride in his work."

Jacques doesn't hold back: "This isn't my work. It's your work. You want to trap me into doing it."

They have had this conversation before. Joseph knows he won't get anywhere with Jacques. But he can't resist going in for one more swat. "We thought you would settle down, find a nice farm girl to be your wife. Instead you are out running around every night with Frenchie and Hungarian Joe. The whole town talks about you. Your mother and I are very disappointed. We're ashamed."

Joseph gets into his truck and drives off. Jacques gives him the finger. He closes the barn door and heads for the house. It is late afternoon, and Frenchie and Hungarian Joe are due anytime.

His partners arrive, and they are sitting at the kitchen table drinking beer. Stacks of dollar bills are spread out on the table. Jacques counts it out and splits it up into three piles. He says, "The minute I have enough saved up, I'm leaving this place. I can't take it. My old man was here today to bitch about the rows in my fields."

Frenchie says, "What do you think. We do three jobs a week. The cigarettes don't pay that much.?

Jacques says, "The booze is better."

Frenchie replies, "After dumping the Chinese over the side, I don't want to do that again. The must have ended up in Toledo, that Detroit River is so fast."

Hungarian Joe whistles: "God damn. That's why they call it Holy Toledo." The three men click their beer bottles and have a hearty laugh.

Jacques says, "It's Saturday night. What do you say we get out of here and find some women."

Jacques, Frenchie, and Hungarian Joe all three sit in the front seat of

Jacques' truck. Jacques is driving. They stop at the Customs booth. The officer waves them on, and they cross the Ambassador Bridge to Detroit. Jacques drive up to a bar all lighted up. Music reverberates out of the door. Jacques parks and they walk in

They step up to the bar. People are drinking, dancing in various stages of inebriation. Women in low-cut dresses hang on some of the men. Girls without men speak loudly to get noticed. The Bartender sets them up.An attractive brunette slinks up next to Jacques. He pats her on the rear. The men all laugh. She grabs his hand and pulls him to the dance floor. Two other women come and grab Frenchie and Hungarian Joe. All three men are now dancing. They came to the right place to pick up women. Jacques is enjoying the frisky brunette who aggressively thrust herself upon him.

He takes it easy with women. He meets them all with rubber gloves. After Shannon and the boys, he has had enough of responsibility. Then there's the woman in town with the little girl she says is his. She can't prove it, and it was part of the game. Her husband is raising the girl. He is into women only for pleasure. Women are into men for marriage, till death do us part, a meal ticket, a roof over their heads, someone to watch over me.

Joseph and Catherine are after him to get a proper farm wife. The"proper" farm wife is Catherine: plain, strong, ugly farm dresses, big black oxfords, a person to work alongside you day after day in the misery of the monotony of the farm. He never even saw Joseph give her a kiss or a hug. He often wondered how they even happened to get him.

Maybe Joseph was drunk. Sometimes, at parties, Joseph will down a few and then he starts grabbing the boobs of girls or reaching up their skirts. They all say, "Here comes Uncle Joe. Hang on to your tits." Then Catherine comes with her big black shoe and kicks him in the ass. No one takes his pinching and grabbing seriously. The whole town holds them up as pillars of the community. He doesn't want a farm. He doesn't want a farm wife. He doesn't want to be a pillar. He wants out. He wants to be free.

It is his idea, as soon as he has saved enough, to move to Montreal. Something tells him that he can create a new life, that he will meet the right people to get him into a good business. He has been there once, and he likes how big it is. McGregor is so small, a one-street town, with everybody paying attention to everything you do, watching you, criticizing you. Well, that's what Joseph said. People are talking about him and Frenchie and Hungarian Joe. There is nothing else to do in McGregor but watch people, talk about people.

So here he is in this low-life bar with this aggressive brunette clinging to him, her boobs pouring out of her blouse, her hips wiggling to come closer. He might as well take advantage of the night. After all, that's why the three of them came here. He might as well take her into the back room and give her what she wants.

He remembers how he did that with Shannon, with that pretty red-head who got tipsy and couldn't stand up after one drop of rum. How crazy was that in the back seat of the car. She was all over him. She wanted it. He gave it to her. Look what it got him. Five years of prison with her and the boys. She wasn't even interesting to talk to. She was pregnant before they ever had a conversation. What does a fifteen-year-old girl have to talk about. She hasn't been anywhere, hasn't done anything.

And those women in town, the ones who play the game. That was to break the boredom of the one-street town, nowhere to go, same man, over and over, till death do us part. That got out of hand, too. The one with the little girl. They were supposed to use rubbers. That was one of the rules. One night he didn't. He didn't know. And he didn't know about Shannon, about Anthony, about Frank. Yes, women are the root of all evil.

This evil one was clawing all over him, panting, spreading her legs. She came into the bar with no pants on. How was that for great expectations! Well, girl, here it is. How do you like that. He hoped Frenchie and Joe were getting it on, too.

Chapter 22

While Vincent was learning to shoot on the farm from his Pippi, he was learning to fish with Mick. His favorite place is on Lake Erie just outside Monroe, Michigan. Mick started taking him there as soon as he moved to Detroit to live with his grandparents. Things have improved for Shannon and the boys. Shannon met a man on the assembly-line, an Italian with a big heart, and she has remarried. His name is Gino. Vincent gave him the silent treatment for a year, but he has finally adjusted to Gino, mainly because of his good cooking.

They only live a couple of blocks away from Mick and Kelly, so Vincent goes back and forth between the two houses. He's thirteen now, just a year away from High School. When he's not at the farm in McGregor, he goes fishing every Sunday. Mick drops him off before he and Kelly go to church and comes back to pick him up at sundown.

On this particular Sunday morning, Mick pulls his 1950 blue Ford up by the shop at the boat dock. They aren't making DeSotos any more. Vincent gets out, opens the back door, and takes out his fishing pole and tackle box. He leans on the front window and says, "Thanks, Gramps."

Mick says, "I'll be back to pick you up at 7," and he drives away.

Vincent goes inside, rents a row boat for the day from the clerk, grabs a pair of oars from the corner, and walks out to the dock. He puts his fishing pole, tackle box, and a pail in the boat and locks the oars in the boat. When he gets to open water, he hooks a lure on to the end of the pole and casts out.

This is pure heaven for Vincent. It puts him in a meditative state, pulling in a fish, putting it in the pail, hooking up the lure, and casting out. He soaks in the sun, the warm air, the beauty of a Michigan day on the lake. He steers his boat to a channel where the fishing is even better. There are trees lining the channel and inlets running off from it. He is concentrating so much on the fishing that he isn't paying attention to the channel or the time of day. He becomes conscious that the sun is going down, and he says to himself, "I'd better turn around now. Gramps will be looking for me."

Vincent turns the boat around and starts back down the channel. It is getting dark, then quite dark. The moon is full and shining down on the channel. This channel leads to another channel, then to another channel. Vincent is confused. He didn't bother to look for landmarks during the afternoon, and now if he knew them he wouldn't be able to see them. He suddenly becomes aware that he hasn't eaten all day and that he's hungry. And now that the sun is down. He is cold. He knows Mick is waiting for him at the dock, and he has no way to let him know that he's lost.

Well, "lost" isn't a word in Vincent's vocabulary. He knows he's on Lake Erie, just a little way from Monroe, in a row boat that he can easily row and steer, in one of the channels off from the lake. It's a whole new experience being out there in the dark. The trees seem even bigger, and in the moonlight, they play tricks on his vision. Well, the trees don't play tricks, but they contribute to the confusion.

Vincent does not like to be confused. Ever since he moved to Detroit, he has felt like he was in control. Shannon was his mother, but she could barely take care of herself. He felt like he was almost as old as she was. And she liked to quarrel. She quarreled all the time with Jacques. Vincent remembers that. But he shouldn't have beaten her, shouldn't have broken her feet, shouldn't have put the gun in her mouth. Vincent is still going to kill him.

He is a really good shot. He can outshoot Pippi. Pippi doesn't wait long enough. He always has to hurry. He doesn't have the sense to calculate how fast the bird is flying, and his bullet always gets there before the bird. Vincent watches, assesses, waits, and hits his target almost every time. He is ready for Jacques when the time comes.

Shannon needed someone to take care of her. He couldn't do it, not with his paper route, *The Detroit Times*. He started delivering the *Times* when he was six. He was finished every morning by 7:00 a.m. Anthony got a paper route, too: *The Detroit Free Press* that comes out in the afternoon. Anthony could never keep his mind on his business. He got out of school, picked up his papers, then played around with his friends. Sometimes he wasn't finished delivering his papers until dark.

Vincent collected every Saturday. When he made his rounds, he stopped at the houses where Anthony delivered the *Free Press*. He asked if they would rather get the *Times*. He promised they would have it by 7:00 a.m. in the morning. He said, "Ask your next door neighbor, Mrs. Clark. She'll tell you how responsible I am." He took people away from Anthony. Then Shannon got mad, because she was always protecting Anthony and making excuses for him.

Finally Shannon met Gino, and they moved into their own house. Shannon and Gino get in a fight every Sunday. That's why Vincent goes fishing. It is really dark now. He knows Mick will be worried. He lets his boat drift up to the shore. Better stay put until morning.

Mick meanwhile has been pacing back and forth on the dock. Calling out "Vincent" got him nowhere. He decides he better just sleep in the car until morning. No one can help him in the dark. He hopes Vincent isn't drowned. He crawls in the back seat and goes to sleep.

Vincent sees someone near the shore, sitting next to a tree that's partially in the water. Vincent pulls the boat all the way to shore and gets out. He walks over to the tree and sees the dead body of a man, partially beginning to decay. He thinks to himself, "He must have been lost, too. I better get out of here." He says to the dead body, "Well, I can't help you, my good man. When I get back to shore, I'll send someone to look for you."

Vincent gets back in his row boat. He doesn't like it on shore, especially with a dead person. Better to stay on the water. The moon is directly overhead. It seems to offer protection. Vincent zips up his jacket and lays down on the floor of the boat. He can hear the fish flopping in the pail.

At dawn, just as there is light, Vincent wakes up and looks around him, attempting to get his bearings. His instinct tells him to follow the current in the channel, to see if that will get him out to the Lake. Where did he ever get that idea? Well, it makes sense. Why didn't he think of it the day before.

The channel opens out to the Lake, just as the sun began to rise. Vincent can see the dock in the distance and begins to row there. Mick sees him coming.

"Damn you, Vincent. I've been scared to death. You've got no business staying out all night like this." Mick is crying.

Vincent says, "I have fish. I found a dead man."

Mick says, "I don't care about fish. I thought you were a dead man."

Chapter 23

Meanwhile, Jacques' intentions are derailed by his libido. It's early afternoon at his farmhouse, and men are unloading boxes from a truck and carrying them into the house. The brunette from the bar is supervising. Another truck pulls up, and Catherine and Joseph get out. They walk up to the porch, and the brunette greets them with a hug and a kiss. We meet Francine.

She says, "Welcome. I am so excited to be settling in. I've baked a cake. Come on in and have some cake and coffee. Jacques will be back in a few minutes."

Joseph and Catherine sit down at the kitchen table, and Francine rustles around, serving them cake and coffee. Jacques walks in and joins them at the table. He comments to his parents, "Well, this is what you wanted. Now I have a wife. Francine likes the farm, and she likes you."

Catherine says, "Let's hope you will bring us a grandchild soon."

Francine says, "We wanted to surprise you. There's one on the way."

Jacques watched the three of them and couldn't help but wonder what would have happened if they had treated Shannon the same way. Here he was doing it to himself all over again. He likes Francine. When he kept going back to the bar on Saturday nights, she was always there. And he got used to her. Then she found out she was pregnant. So here he is again, another woman, another child on the way. Only this time he has a farm and a house. Joseph and   Catherine got just what they wanted.

Francine does throw herself into being a farm wife. When he is out on the tractor, she brings him his lunch. She plants a vegetable garden to raise food for the kitchen. She plants flowers: tulips and lilac bushes and roses. She loves to cook and to have people over. She invites Hungarian Joe and Frenchie to dinner one night every week. She invites Joseph and Catherine. She changes things around in the house, moves furniture, makes curtains, paints walls.

When she has the little girl, Jacques enjoys having a daughter. It is different from boys. He liked Vincent, liked taking him in the truck, taking him down to the barn, taking him out in the field hunting. But with a little girl, he feels as if he wants to protect her. Francine makes her cute little dresses, dresses her up like a doll.

They are playing house and farm. His rows are a little straighter. Joseph and Catherine are happy. So he will never get to Montreal, never get to the bigger life. He has shelved that dream. He still has money set aside. He and Frenchie and Hungarian Joe still do their thing, but only once a week now. He has worked at convincing himself that this is the life he is meant to live.

Yet Francine is getting on his nerves. She wants to have another baby. She wants her parents to move to McGregor and live near them. She wants her sister to come and stay. She wants to paint the outside of the house. She wants a new rug in the living room. She wants, she wants, she wants. Every time he comes into the house from the field, she wants something else.

He starts going out at night with Frenchie and Hungarian Joe more often. He is happier doing his small-time smuggling than he is at home. The more he is away, the more demanding Francine becomes. She talks about him to his parents. She talks to people around McGregor, complaining. She is getting too cozy with too many people. She wants more and more money for the house, for their daughter, for her parents. That old feeling he had with Shannon is coming back. He has trapped himself in another prison with a dissatisfied woman. Could a woman ever be satisfied? Could he ever be satisfied?

He does like Elsie, the little girl. When he comes in from the fields, she runs to him squealing. He swoops her up in his arms, and she gives him a slobbery kiss. She does the same thing for Frenchie and Hungarian Joe. Neither of them has to put up with Francine in order to have Elsie. Were all women the same? He doesn't remember Catherine making demands. But then her father gave them the farm. Jacques hasn't thought of it before, but that put Catherine in control. Yes, his mother is in control. Is that what all women want, control?

It is all coming to a head. He is ready to explode. Then one Saturday afternoon, he does. He has been out on a "job" for three days with the guys. It's the biggest haul they have ever made. It is building their confidence. He is always happy doing that, and he always dreads going home. Today is no different.

When he walks in, Elsie is playing on the kitchen floor. She has pots and pans on the floor, and she is banging on them with a big wooden spoon. She gets up and runs to Jacques, expecting her hug. She wants to be thrown in the air. She cries out, "Daddy, Daddy." Why doesn't Jacques like that word?

Francine stands by the stove. She glares at him.

"Where have you been? We've been alone here for three days. Your folks have been here twice looking for you."

Jacques says, "It's none of your business."

Francine says, "Then whose business is it? I'm your wife." It is always in the back of Francine's mind how she met Jacques. He came to the same bar as she did every Saturday night. She pursued him. She found him handsome. He always seemed to have enough money. She wanted a husband.

But she has been talking around town. She has met a woman named Dolly who knew Shannon, still keeps in touch with her. She has heard rumors about the neighbor's little girl, and a sex game they used to play in town. Was Jacques playing that game again? Was he going back to the bar? What kind of business did he and Frenchie and Hungarian Joe have on the side? She was Jacques' wife, and he knew everything about her. She didn't know anything about him.

Jacques, enraged by Francine's nagging, slaps her in the face. She begins to cry. Elsie, sitting on the floor, begins to cry.

Jacques screams, "What I do is my business, none of your business. I'm sick of you, sick of this farm, sick of this town. I can't stand you!"

Somehow, Francine had been expecting this. She cries out, "Is that what happened to the first one? Dolly told me about her, told me about the boys, told me they had to escape to Detroit because you beat her. And now you are beating me."

Jacques yells, "Why are you talking to Dolly? She's a tramp."

Francine screams, "I want to know what I got myself into. She fills me in. Other people know, too. There are no secrets in McGregor."

Jacques picks up a butcher knife and starts toward her. He is shaking with anger.

Francine runs, gather up Elsie off the floor, breaks through the back door on to the porch. She jumps off the porch, holding the child. Jacques is chasing her. She opens the truck door, throws Elsie in, and gets in the driver's seat. She starts up the truck and screeches out of the driveway, just as Jacques gets to the truck. She heads toward Joseph and Catherine's farm.

PART 2

Chapter 24

So now Jacques is free from that one, too. Francine filed for divorce. She didn't want to hold on for another attack. Actually Catherine and Joseph helped her. They were very concerned about the well-being of Elsie. Jacques doesn't escape child support this time. Francine's lawyer is better than Shannon's. He does not ask for visitation rights with Elsie, only for his parents. The truth is, he doesn't want to be bothered with kids.

Now he is back on track for escaping the farm prison. The second marriage derailed his scheme for getting to Montreal, but now nothing stands in his way except money. For the past three months he has been doing little jobs for a diamond merchant in Detroit on his own, no Frenchie, sometimes including Hungarian Joe when he needs him. The merchant has built up a level of trust with Jacques even though Jacques isn't Jewish. Jews don't do this sort of business.

When he stops by on Tuesday morning, he is surprised that the merchant has a slightly bigger job for him. He takes an unopened box out of the showcase and puts it on the counter. He says, "I need to get this to my brother in Toronto. Can you do it for me? He has a showroom there, and he needs it by Thursday." Jacques says, "That's my business. Who pays me?"

The merchant says, "I will pay you. This will be a bag exchange. I'll put the merchandise in a bag for you to deliver to my brother. He will give you a bag to return to me. When I get his bag, you get paid."

Jacques says, "Well, you have always come through so far, so I will trust you. If I pick it up tomorrow morning. I can have it to him by Thursday and back to you by Saturday. Is that good enough?"

The merchant sticks out his hand for the hand-shake. It's on.

Jacques is back as soon as the store opens the next day. The merchant hands him a small sealed bag, and Jacques heads out the door and gets into his truck, JACQUES PASCAL BUTCHER. The bag is so small, he can put it in the inner pocket of his jacket. The officer at the end of the bridge just waves him by.

As soon as he is across the bridge, he heads for his farmhouse to examine the seal. He wants to get it off to see what's in the bag before he delivers it. The seal is wax. He has to figure out how to melt it enough to open the bag and then re-seal it so it won't show. He heats a silver knife in a pot of boiling water and lightly touches the wax. It's just enough heat to cause the wax to soften enough for him to split it, without defacing the seal. Jacques pours the content of the bag on the counter – 15 gems, all diamonds, of various sizes. He examines them carefully. Assuming the brother will be sending back something similar, he needs to find matching glass beads in Toronto.

He puts the gems back in the bag, puts the knife back in the boiling water, and melts the wax enough to close the seal. He knows the two brothers will talk as soon as he makes the first delivery, and he wants it to be impeccable. Jacques gets in his truck and heads down the road. He stops by to see Hungarian Joe to tell him he may need him on Saturday. Then he's on his way toward Toronto. He will spend the night there so he has enough time to find the beads. He can just sleep in his truck.

The next morning Jacques pulls his truck up to a shop on a busy Toronto street. It's much more up-scale than the one in Detroit. He always thought the Jew in Detroit had some other business going on in the back room, but it was enough for him that the guy paid him when he did a job. He didn't ask questions.

The man behind the counter here in Toronto looks like his brother. Jacques introduces himself. No one else is in the shop. Jacques takes the bag out of his jacket, hands it to the man. He inspects the seal. Then he reaches into the showcase and takes out another small bag, also sealed with wax, and hands it to Jacques. They shake hands, and Jacques leaves.

Jacques drives down the street, into a less up-scale area, where there are several jewelry stores all in a row. He stops by three of them before he finds one that has loose glass beads for sale that look like diamonds. They are more expensive than he expected, but he buys 40 of them, various sizes. He has to make this work. Then he gets into his truck and heads back to McGregor.

So there he is, Friday night, back at the farmhouse. Hungarian Joe stops by to find him with a pile of glass beads on one side of the counter. Jacques is boiling water to heat the knife to warm the wax on the seal. He is feeling like an old pro. Hungarian Joe is in awe when he empties the bag on the other side of the counter. The Jacques begins very methodically matching glass bead with diamond, glass bead with diamond. Each match he makes, he puts the glass bead in the merchant's bag and the diamond in his own bag. It's important he bought so many. He heats the knife, seals the wax.

When he's finished, he goes to the cupboard and takes out a whiskey bottle. He pours himself and Hungarian Joe each a glass of whiskey. They clink and drink, and Jacques says, "This is our ticket out of town. It can't come soon enough. I'm on my second divorce. I need to get away from this farm and out of this prison."

Hungarian Joe is the sort of guy who will always go along for the ride. He's not as smart as Jacques. But he has been smart enough to stay away from the woman trap. He has always thought Jacques should keep his pants zipped, but he hasn't said anything. If Jacques wants to go somewhere else, and if he wants him to come along, he's ready. He just does odd jobs in McGregor and the smuggling on the side with Jacques and Frenchie.

Hungarian Joe has a little money saved up. He has a girlfriend he sort of likes, but not enough to get married. He lives at his mother's house. She's a widow. She doesn't pay attention to what he's doing. In fact, he thinks her memory is starting to go. But they don't talk much. She's Hungarian, from the old country. She never forgets she is Hungarian. If someone comes to the door, the first thing she says is, "We're Hungarian." No wonder he got stuck with the name "Hungarian Joe."

His mother would never let him forget it. She's a kind of dark cloud hanging over him. If he can get away, why not. He can't help commenting to Jacques, however, about what people say about him: "Everyone in this town thinks you've got it made – a farm, a slaughter house, a butcher business, parents who always think you're right. Even when we were in college, you always had money when the rest of us didn't. We all thought you were spoiled, but we liked your company and what you did with your money."

Jacques responds, "My parents don't know me. They only know the farm, work from morning to night, day after day, week after week, month after month, year after year. Their idea of a great time is a game of cards on Saturday night."

Then Jacques begins to instruct Hungarian Joe on their plans for Saturday, where he's supposed to be and when, what he's supposed to do. Jacques can't pull this off alone. He is psyched. He loves it when he has that feeling, the adrenalin flow.

Chapter 25

At 8:30 the next morning, Jacques goes out of the farmhouse. He has the bag of glass beads tucked inside his jacket. He puts the bag of diamonds in the recess under his truck where they carry the cigarettes. Hungarian Joe has spent the night. He watches Jacques get into his truck.

Jacques has instructed him what he's to do. He drives to the slaughter house and goes in. Joseph never locks it. He gets out a butcher smock and puts it in his car. He opens the car trunk. Then he goes back into the slaughter house and takes down a side of beef. He puts that in the trunk. Jacques has instructed him to be waiting at the foot of the Bridge at 9:30.

Jacques knows the merchant in Detroit always opens at 9:00 a.m. He wants to be there before anyone comes into the shop. He drives up to the showroom, parks his truck, and walks in. The merchant greets him: "You're right on time. Do you have the goods?" He has spoken with his brother in Toronto. The bag was delivered without the seal broken. Nothing in the bag was disturbed. Jacques has proved himself trustworthy.

Jacques takes the bag out of his jacket and hands it to the merchant. He examines the seal, opens the bag, and pours out the "gems" on the black velvet on the counter. He smiles. Then he goes to the cash register and takes out the pile of $100 bills he has waiting. He counts it out. "$10,000 as agreed." He puts the cash in a bag and hands it to Jacques.

Jacques shakes his hand and leaves the shop. He gets into his truck and drives away, thinking, "That went a lot better than I thought it would. Whew!"

The merchant starts to put away the "gems," and then, out of habit, picks up one to examine with his device. Then he picks up a second, and a third. "God damn son-of-a-bitch. These are not diamonds. The fucker robbed me." The merchant goes to the phone on the wall and dials. He's calling the police to alert the Bridge. He is sure Jacques will be going back to Canada as a get-away.

"This is Erwin at Quality Diamonds. I just got robbed by a Canadian in a truck that's headed over the Bridge. He stole diamonds from me. It's a black Ford truck with a flat bed and wooden slats on the side. It has JACQUES PASCAL BUTCHER on the door. He's wearing a black jacket."

Erwin is right. Jacques is headed straight for the Bridge. He stops at Customs. The Customs officer waves him through. Half way across the Bridge, he pulls over and stops his truck. He gets out and crawls under the truck, taking the bag of diamonds out of the hiding place in the recess. He tucks the bag of diamonds inside his jacket, gets back in the truck, and drives away.

He is almost at the end of the Bridge when he sees a Police car behind him. The officer turns on the siren, motions for him to pull over. Jacques turns the truck sideways and parks it so that it blocks the Bridge. He takes the keys out of the ignition and grabs the bag of cash. He gets out of the truck and starts climbing the scaffold, up to the top of the

Bridge. The police officer fires. Another police car pulls up, and two more officers get out. They start shooting at Jacques.

Jacques is at the top of the Bridge. It's narrow, but he can walk along it. The officers are shooting, and he is going as fast as he can. He is out of their fire range. The bullets won't go that high. Jacques gets to the end of the Bridge, climbs down the scaffold to reach the bottom. Hungarian Joe is waiting with his car.

Jacques says, "The cops are right behind me. They've been shooting. It will only be a few minutes before they can get around my truck." They drive away.

Meanwhile two of the policemen are at Jacques' truck. One sits in the driver's seat. The other one has the hood up. He is crossing the wires. The truck starts up. The officer in the driver's seat turns it around and moves it over to the side of the Bridge. He gets out of the truck and climbs into the Police car. The two Police cars are now leaving the Bridge, heading down the road toward McGregor.

Hungarian Joe is checking the rear view mirror. "God damn, they're not behind us yet."

Jacques says, "They will have to deal with my truck blocking the Bridge."

Hungarian Joe's car passes the WELCOME TO McGREGOR sign, proceeds down the main street, and drives behind the Golden Boar Restaurant next to the hotel. They park the car.

The Police have their siren on. One of them comments, "The guy's a clever bastard."

The other officer replies, "We'll catch him in town. This is a one-street town. There's nowhere to go, nowhere to hide."

Jacques and Hungarian Joe get out of the car. Hungarian Joe opens the back door and takes out the butcher smock he put in the back seat. He helps Jacques put it on. He opens the trunk, and Jacques takes out the side of beef, slings it over his shoulder. He heads in the back door of the restaurant.

The police park their car and go into the Hotel. Men are standing at the bar. The police look around for Jacques. They go up to the bartender:

"Has some guy in a black jacket just come in here?"

The bartender says, "These guys have been here for more than an hour. We haven't seen anyone else. It's been pretty quiet this morning."

The officer who asked says, "Thanks. We'll try the restaurant. He may have gone in there."

People have gathered along the street in McGregor. It isn't often that a police car with a siren comes crashing through the town. They're all curious. They watch the two police officers go next door and enter the Golden Boar." Just as they go to the front desk to ask if a man in a black jacket has just come in, Jacques in his butcher smock comes from the kitchen of the restaurant with the side of beef on his back. He passes the two police officers and goes out the front door.

Hungarian Joe has pulled up from behind the restaurant. He stops and opens the trunk. Jacques slides the side of beef off from his shoulder and puts it in the trunk. He closes the trunk. The two men get into the car. They are slow and methodical. There is no hurry, no need to call attention to themselves from the people along the street watching for the police.

Jacques is driving Hungarian Joe's car. "We made it."

"Damn," says Hungarian Joe, "that was a close call."

They head out of town, on the road to Montreal. There's no going back now. Jacques has the $10,000 cash and the bag of diamonds. They will ransack McGregor and won't find him. The merchant in Detroit doesn't know where he lives. All he knows is the truck with JACQUES PASCAL BUTCHER, and that life is history. Catherine and Joseph don't have, won't have a clue. Someday he'll get in touch with them again. Not now.

Chapter 26

Vincent has just turned 14 and has moved beyond the *Detroit Times*. First he set pins at the bowling alley, then he got a job at the local grocery store, Stein and Stein. It's a one-stop Mom and Pop with everything from booze to a first-class meat department overseen by the butcher. Owned by Sadie and Abe Stein, the meat is the best in Detroit, or at least in Lincoln Park. Vincent was hired to stock shelves and sweep the floors, but once in a while Sadie even lets him run the cash register. He's so good at everything he does that Sadie has asked, "Are there any more boys at school like you?"

Sadie has a special fondness for Vincent because at Christmas he brought her a brooch, all wrapped up in Christmas paper and tied with a ribbon. Sadie said, "I can't take a Christmas present. We're Jews." Vincent said, "Well, you may not celebrate Christmas, but we do. And at Christmas, we give gifts. So I wanted to bring this to you, and you must accept it."

Sadie opened her box, looked in at the ornate brooch, and began to cry. She was so touched by this thoughtful boy who always did everything he was told. She overlooked that she caught him in the walk-in refrigerator with the whipped cream can pointed right into his mouth. Vincent said, "Close the door. Can't you see I'm busy." That's what she and Abe liked about him – always thinking on his feet and making her laugh. She can't get mad at him.

On this particular afternoon, Vincent has finished sweeping the aisles of the store and is stocking shelves by the meat counter. Now Sadie is almost as wide as she is tall, and she is bending over. Vincent can't help himself. He pulls a slingshot out of his pocket and shoots her on the butt. Sadie turns around to see who did it, sees the butcher behind the meat counter, and screams at him: "Why did you do that."

The butcher replies, "It wasn't me. It was the boy."

The butcher comes around from behind the meat counter and starts to chase Vincent for Sadie. Vincent is running down the aisle, faster than either of them. He is running so fast, the butcher can't catch him, and he is huffing and puffing. Vincent slides behind the meat counter, picks up the knife, and starts cutting the side of beef the butcher has laid out for himself. Abe is laughing and comes behind the meat counter to watch.

One of the things Pippie has taught Vincent is how to cut meat. He took him out to the slaughter house and demonstrated that the key to being a good butcher is to start with a sharp knife. They stood side by side, knives in hand, beginning with the loin, and working through the entire side. Pippie didn't do it just once. They have practiced over and over. When Vincent puts that sharp knife in his hand, he goes on automatic. Vincent has become so adept Catherine will tell him to go out to the slaughter house and bring her a rump roast to cook for dinner.

So Vincent, laughing too, is totally absorbed with his task. Abe cries out to the exhausted butcher, "Hey, butcher, come here and watch this boy cut meat."

The butcher comes round the counter, both of them now

watching. "Damn, says the butcher. He's as good as I am."

Abe says, "Vincent, no more stocking shelves. You are now a butcher."

Vincent knows there's a big gap between the pay for stocking shelves and butcher's wages, especially Union wages. Vincent's grandfather, Mick, has taught him a thing or two. He says, "Union wages?"

Abe replies "Union wages! But first I need to show you how to weigh a chicken."

Vincent looks on while Abe puts a chicken on the scale. Then, out of sight from the other side of the meat counter, Abe lowers a piece of liver on a string above the scale and drops it on the chicken. He registers the weight and the price. Then he lets the liver go back up and wraps the package. All the customer can see from the other side of the meat counter is the weight and the price.

Abe announces, "Now that's the way to weigh a chicken."

Vincent laughs and says, "Here, let me try it." He goes through the procedure while Abe and the butcher look on. His performance is perfect.

Abe says, "You will make a fine butcher. Take the rest of the day off."

Vincent is beside himself with joy. He shakes hands with Abe and the butcher, hugs Sadie, and heads out of the store. Who would have thought that would happen when he shot Sadie in the butt. He leaves Stein and Stein, jumps on his bike, and pedals over to the front of the Clancy home. His grandfather, Mick, is raking leaves in front of the house. A neighbor across the street is washing his car at the curb. Vincent salutes Mick and says, "Guess what, Gramps. I just got promoted. I am now a butcher."

Mick says, "Union wages?"

Vincent shouts, the triumph pouring out of his voice, "Union wages!"

He is so loud that the neighbor hears the conversation and stops washing his car. He crosses the street, greets them both, and says to Vincent, "Well, now that you're a butcher, buy this car." He points to the blue Chrysler sedan he has been washing at the curb. It is a beautiful, long, sleek car.

Mick says, "How much?"

The neighbor replies, "$800."

Mick says, "We'll take a look." He and Vincent cross the street with the neighbor. Vincent gets into the car, and Mick lifts the hood. He bangs around in there, checking things out. You can't fool a good Ford mechanic like Mick.

Mick says, "Sold."

Vincent says, "Gramps, I don't have $800."

Mick says, "I'll loan it to you. You can pay me $25 a week until it's yours."

Vincent is jumping up and down. He hugs Mick. He hugs the neighbor. All in one day he has gone from stocking shelves to being a butcher, to owning a car – or to buying a car.

Actually, he already has his driver's license, the Farmer's License you can get at 14. When he went down to apply for the license, the officer took him out into the parking lot for the driver's test. Vincent told him he helped his grandfather on his farm. He said to Vincent, before they were ready to drive away: "Well, son, what else do you know how to drive?"

Vincent said, "Well, I can drive a tractor, a manure spreader, a plow, a combine, a fertilizer spreader, a baler."

"Stop!" exclaimed the officer. "That's enough. You do not even need to go out of the driveway. Here's your license."

Pippie has done a pretty good job getting Vincent ready for the next step. He has let Vincent do everything on the farm and in the slaughter house. He has trained him the same way he trained his own son, letting him learn anything he wants to learn. The difference is that Vincent takes to it, loves all of it. Now Vincent will be able to drive himself across the Bridge to the farm in his own car whenever he has time.

Chapter 27

Jacques and Hungarian Joe made it to Montreal. Frenchie was waiting for them at the side of the road at the edge of McGregor, and the three of them went together. The police scoured McGregor to find Jacques. They went to Jacques' farm, to Catherine and Joseph's farm. His parents didn't know anything about anything. This business on the side was never mentioned. The truck with JACQUES PASCAL BUTCHER on the side was confiscated by the police and taken to Detroit. It wasn't exactly a closed case because the diamonds were still missing. But since they were loose stones, it was impossible to trace them, and Jacques was smart enough to sell each one individually to a different jeweler.

They cleaned up well, especially Jacques. He was a handsome man, dark hair, muscular from all of the work on the farm, penetrating brown eyes, and an infectious smile and laugh. In his bib overhauls, he looked like a farmer. He was a farmer. When he put on a business suit, he became a business man. It was natural for him.

After all, farming is a business. The slaughter house was a business. Joseph couldn't read, but he could bargain and he could strategize. When the price of soybeans went down, he built silos for the soybeans and the next year sold them as seed – making far more money. He built the silo in a V so the seeds would flow out the bottom. Since he was a teenager, Jacques had been given the hides to sell. He knew how to read faces, how to make demands, how to calculate responses, how to wait for the order.

Montreal was a lively city, totally divided between the Haves and the Have-Nots. Many different immigrant groups flocked there from the Old World. They hung out together. None of the jobs they could get paid enough money to support one person, let alone a family. So the only way to make enough money to support a family was to steal and to sell. Like all other groups, hierarchies developed, the smartest leading the pack, telling the rest what to do, skimming off passive profit from the work of others.

Jacques took his time exploring these groups, staying on the fringe, observing the hierarchy, surmising the quality of the leadership at the top, the effectiveness of the organization – the Irish, the Italian, the French. He spoke French. That was convenient. The McGregor French was not exactly city French, but he was smart enough to eliminate certain words and phrases from his conversation that would give him away.

While he was doing that, he was setting himself, Joe and Frenchie up in business. He had enough money accumulated from the sale of the diamonds to buy into something big, something that would make money. He didn't intend to work for anyone. He wanted to be in business for himself. He brought Joe and Frenchie alongside because he liked them. He also knew the importance of the people you can trust, the ones you can count on one hand, the ones that cover your back and look out for you. The ones who will do what you ask without questioning you.

It took a while to sell the diamonds. He had the $10,000 and the savings from the three of them so that he could take his time. They could live well, show up well, establish a presence as someone to know. In a city with so many new people coming in all the time, it wasn't unusual for an "unknown" to become someone desirable to "know." That's how Jacques held himself. He had time to wait for the best opportunity.

His choices weren't unlimited, rather they were limited. He wasn't looking for anything legitimate. He had enough "legitimate" business on the farm. The money was in the illegitimate - the gambling, the prostitution, the booze. He actually enjoyed horse racing, organized gambling with a little race-fixing on the side. He found himself down at the tracks every afternoon. His favorite was the Blue Bonnet.

There you could make money on the horses, money on the gambling, money on the liquor and food – money to be made everywhere you turned. There was plenty for all of them to do. He got himself introduced to the owners, started hanging out with them, betting just enough to get their attention. Then he raised the question - did they want to sell.

Maybe yes, maybe no. There were three of them. They were all making good money. The business was running well. They suggested Jacques buy in with them. Jacques considered. They negotiated. They talked. He hesitated. He liked them ok, but he needed to be in charge. No other way.

He had planted the seed. Once you plant the seed of selling, it doesn't just dry up from lack of water. It starts to send out roots. You start thinking about how it might be if you didn't have to be there every day, if you took your wife to Europe, if you bought a yacht and went fishing, if you moved to Florida and didn't have to contend with the raw winters, if you could get away from the kind of people who hang out around race tracks: the smoke, the smell of booze, the smell of sweat from the ones who are losing and won't go home.

Jacques had waited long enough. He made his move. What if he
bought them out but let them stay in for a slice as his partners. In other
words, the Blue Bonnet would be his to run as he wished, and they would
be able to lay claim to passive income. One condition: They could not
be part of the day-to-day operation. They talked among themselves.
They went home and talked to their wives. They were not young men.
They had been "tied to the track" for years.

They came back. They had a price. Jacques thought it was too
high. He wanted to examine the books. Forget that. The money to be
made was off the books. They had estimates. How would they know if
he was paying them enough? How would they keep track of him? It
wouldn't work. Everyone would be suspicious of everyone else.

So what if Jacques bought them out for the higher price, gave them
60% in cash, and they carried the rest over 10 years. He would pay each
of them every month, principal plus interest, until the debt would be paid
off. Jacques would take out a life insurance policy on each of them for
twice what he owed them with himself as the beneficiary. They would
each pay for the policy out of the proceeds from the 60% up-front cash.

Jacques' experience with the insurance business was not wasted on
him. This made the loan a wager. If the seller lived the next ten years,
he would get his money plus interest, paid every month. If the seller died
before the debt was paid off, Jacques would collect twice the sum he
"borrowed" with interest. He would then honor the remainder of the
debt with payments to the widow, but he would keep the entire pay-out

of the insurance company.

Jacques was not in a hurry. He kept the end in mind. The insurance policy was no skin off their back. He was betting they wouldn't live ten years, but whether they did or didn't, they still received the agreed amount. They felt as if they were being "had," a legitimate illegitimate, but logic didn't prove it. They came to agreement, signed the contracts, bought the insurance policies, and all shook hands. Jacques was the new owner of the Blue Bonnet after only eighteen months in Montreal. Too bad he couldn't tell anyone still back on the farm. They wouldn't understand anyway.

Chapter 28

It's late afternoon on a Saturday when Vincent, age 15, drives his blue Chrysler into the farmyard in McGregor. He just got off work from Stein and Stein and decided to cross the Bridge to his grandparents' farm. With his wages as a butcher, he is able to afford the tuition at St. Patrick's, and he is in the ninth grade in High School there. The nun who teaches his biology class has asked him for help.

As he pulls into the barnyard, he sees Joseph standing by the barn. So he parks, gets out and walks over to his grandfather: "Hello, Pippi." He gives him a warm hug.

Joseph says, "I still can't believe you drive yourself over here. It seems like yesterday when I put you on a tractor for the first time and gave you your shotgun."

"Well, Pippi, it's because of you and the farm that I got my license so early. I didn't even need to take the driver's test. It sure is great having my own wheels. And it means I can come and visit whenever I get hungry for Mimi's cooking."

"She'll be glad to feed you," says Pippi. "Should we head on up to the house? I would love to ride in your car."

Vincent says, "Sure. But before we go, I hope you can help me with a school project." Then he proceeds to tell his grandfather about his Biology class and how the nun wants them to dissect something. He didn't exactly promise, but he told her he thought he could help. He had the idea that maybe he could shoot the crows in the barnyard and take them to school. There are always hundreds of crows hanging around the farm, and when they gather in one place, he figures he could shoot them.

Joseph says, "We just butchered a hog. I know how to bring them in. The best time is in the morning. Can you spend the night?"

Vincent says, "Sure. I wouldn't miss Mimi's cooking. Hop in, Pippi, and I'll give you a ride up to the house."

The two of them climb into the blue Chrysler, and Vincent drives up to the house, honking the horn. Mimi comes out on the porch, excited to see him. She is wearing the usual - a long housedress, thick black oxfords and an apron. She is drying her hands on her apron. This is a woman who works from dawn to dusk.

Vincent jumps out of the car and runs up on the porch to greet her. She stretches out her arms in joy. She says, "Well, I'll be, you're just in time for supper."

Mimi always has enough food for an army, even when it's just her and Joseph. That's why his stomach keeps getting bigger and bigger, and he always needs a nap after he eats. It's her Saturday night special meatloaf with mashed potatoes, and she beams as she watches Vincent devour her food and wash it down with the tumbler of wine he filled on his way into the house.

He tells them stories about his new school, St. Patrick's, where they only take the best students from the various schools across Detroit. Now that Vincent has the car, he can drive there, and he picks up a couple of other students on the way who pay for the gas. He's on the football team, and so far Father Donnoley, who heads the school, and the nuns really like him. It's always important for Vincent to have people like him.

He is taking Math and English and History, but his favorite class is Biology, and his favorite nun, Sister Francis, is the teacher. That's why he wants to get the crows. Joseph explains that the very best time is just after the sun comes up. The crows gather then, and they always call each other when they find something good. It's one of the finer qualities of crows: They share.

So the next morning, Vincent and Joseph are in the slaughter house next to the barn. They are filling pails with pig guts out of a huge vat. They carry the pails out into the field by the barn and dump the guts in a pile. After two trips, the crows start to gather and to call each other. Vincent and Joseph make five trips, so the heap of guts is huge. It is a symphony of "Caw, Caw, Caw" as the crowd grows.

Vincent takes his shotgun and climbs up to the top of the hay mow in the barn. He opens the door and looks out directly upon the crows. Vincent shoots, and the buckshot sprays out on the crows. They drop dead. Vincent shoots again. More drop dead. He keeps shooting until there is a pile of dead crows on top of the guts. Something happens inside him – a feeling of triumph, of accomplishment, of grandiosity, larger than life. It's a good feeling, one that he wants to keep happening.

Vincent gathers some gunny sacks out of the barn and goes out into the middle of the dead crows. He starts to fill them. Joseph stands on the side-lines and watches, actually filled with pride to see his grandson perform so effectively. He has been his teacher. He would make a fine farmer, better than his father ever would. But then, who knows what Vincent will do. He's an unusual boy.

Vincent carries the gunny sacks to his car and fills the trunk. He goes back to the house, hugs his grandparents, and gets in and drives off. When he gets to the Ambassador Bridge, he stops at the Guard stand. The Customs Officer says, "Anything to declare?"

Vincent gets out and opens the trunk. "Dead crows."

The Customs Officer says, "Dead crows. What are you going to do with them?

Vincent says, "Crow pies,"

The Customs Officer says, "Get outa here!" and waves him on. He is laughing.

On Monday morning Vincent pulls into the parking lot at St. Patrick's. Biology is his first class. He asks the two boys who ride with him to help him carry the gunny sacks into the school. Sister Francis is at her desk when they walk in. Vincent says, "Here are your crows."

Sister Francis is jumping up and down. She looks into the sacks. She can't believe that he actually did it. When the bell rings, the students pour into the classroom and sit down at the desk. Sister Francis leads them in the Pledge of Allegiance and a prayer. She ends the prayer by thanking God for helping Vincent bring a crow for every student in the class.

She asks Vincent to help her put one crow on each desk. The girls are giggling and shrieking at the very idea of even touching the crows. Another student is helping Sister pass out sharp knives, one for each student in the class. Then Sister Francis goes to the blackboard and draws the inside of the crow, labeling each organ and explaining the function of each one.

She clears the front of her desk and puts a dead crow right in the middle. She lifts her knife, and she makes the central incision, demonstrating what she expects each student to do. She pulls the feathers aside, opens the incision. She asks each student to file past, to see what they will see with their own crow. When they return to their seats, she tells them to begin. She walks up and down the aisles, supervising.

Vincent is receiving notes from the other students, especially the girls. "I hate you, Vincent." "Vincent, you are a crow murderer." "Vincent, keep your crows down on the farm." "Vincent, you will do anything to be teacher's pet."

Vincent smiles. It's a good day. He has already made his incision.

Chapter 29

With the purchase of the Blue Bonnet sealed, Jacques has established himself as a businessman in Montreal. He and Frenchie and Hungarian Joe have moved into the offices and begun learning the ropes of both running a race track and manipulating the betting. Part of the agreement with the former owners was that they would stay and train them before they left. They also agreed to educate them in making betting profitable both within the law and on the fringes of the law.

Jacques is comfortable with the fringes. That's where he's always been. He has a manner that draws people to him, a kind of confidence that is contagious, and a winning way of greeting people and telling stories. He is an attractive man, especially dressed as he is now, in suits and ties and white shirts with his initials on the cuffs and gold cuff links. When he walks into a room, he takes over.

Frenchie and Hungarian Joe have never questioned his leadership, never questioned that they work for Jacques. From the first small smuggling operations, he was the instigator, the strategist, the decision maker, the prime mover. When something was going wrong, he would immediately order them to pull back, to let it go. They left it to Jacques to calculate.

They are making good money now. Jacques not only gives them a salary, he gives them a piece of the action from the betting, a percentage. For Jacques, it is a motivator to encourage them to hustle, and it is also a tie to their loyalty, not that he doesn't trust them. Jacques is always cautious, always holding back the best cards in his hand.

His knowledge of the insurance business is never out of his consciousness. It enters into his practice. Just as he used it to purchase the Blue Bonnet, he has the operation broken down into insurable components. Frenchie and Hungarian Joes are two of the components. He is the beneficiary to life insurance policies on both of them. No need to take chances.

Jacques has been in Montreal long enough now to evaluate the "families" and to identify the one he wishes to join. You don't just walk in and declare a desire to be part of the clan. You begin with one or two of the insiders, getting to know them on the outside.

His choice is the DuBois family. Their origin is French. His first language is French. He has some French ways about him even from his small town upbringing on the farm. And his taste for everything exceeds the farm – for food, for wine, for gambling, for women.

Two of the brothers hang out at the tracks. Jacques got to know them, inviting them for a drink, giving them occasional tips on the horses, asking them to lunch in the restaurant. They own one of the high-end Clubs in Montreal, the Carat Club, a prime location for the business in the backroom and the women in the front. They have invited Jacques to the Club a few times. He has been careful not to sample the goods.

He has a higher goal. The two brothers have a sister, Collette, a known and sought-after beauty in Montreal. Jacques has foolishly allowed his zipper to rule him in the past, with two disastrous marriages in McGregor, one brief "encounter" annulled in Montreal. He's not going to make that mistake again. Any future marriage will be pre-meditated, calculated, weighed for optimum gain. He wants money, he wants prestige, he wants to be part of a "family."

Collette has joined them at the club a couple of times. She often comes in with her mother in the late afternoon, after they have had lunch together nearby. Her father has been dead for five years, so the brothers run the family business, advise the mother, make the decisions for her. It is pretty much unsaid that they don't wander outside the "family." They hold things close.

Jacques can feel that Collette finds him attractive, that she maneuvers to sit next to him at the table, that she asserts herself into the conversation, even flirts with him. The brothers have noticed. Collette is a "family" commodity, one closely held, not to be flagrantly marketed. Any man who marries Collette will become one of them, one of the family. They all work together, do business together, live together on the same street. Even though your last name may not be DuBois, you are DuBois when you marry into that family.

Jacques is subtle, never pushy. He only stops by the Club when he is invited. He always leaves before they want him to leave. He always insists on paying his way. After all, the brothers pay for their bets when they come to the Blue Bonnet. He demonstrates that he contributes to the business, is not a drain on the business.

The big break comes when they invite him to Christmas Dinner. He brings every member of the "family" a gift, the mother, the brothers, their wives, their children. For Collette, he selects a stunning necklace of rubies that complements her dark hair and eyes. Her favorite color is red. When she opens it she blushes, her face turns red. He has broken the family seal. It is now "open" courtship.

As he enters more and more into the family gatherings, he is being given permission. The sister-in-laws invite him to dinner. He plays with the children, throws them up in the air, enters into hide and seek, kick the can, whatever games they are playing. The children are calling him "Uncle Jacques."

It seems only natural that he should be a permanent member of the "family," that he should marry Collette. She is sending him clear signals, touching him with signs of affection, always sitting next to him at the table, hanging on his every word, always making sure that he is included.

So, Jacques knows it is time. He speaks to the brothers. Does he have their permission to marry Collette if she will have him? They say they need to discuss it. They ask about the Blue Bonnet. If he were to marry a DuBois, would the Blue Bonnet become a part of the DuBois "family" dynasty, or would he hold it independently? Would his wife assume joint ownership? In the end, everything comes down to money. Love is secondary, even tertiary.

Jacques tells them everything is negotiable. He explains that he made a cash down payment on the track, that he has debts. He explains that two of his employees, Hungarian Joe and Frenchie, have been with him for many years. They come with him no matter what he does. The brothers respect his loyalty. They want the same for their sister.

Jacques does not reveal that he has been married twice before, had a third marriage annulled, that he has three sons by his first wife, a daughter by his second, and an illegitimate daughter in McGregor. His past has no place in Montreal. His past has no place in his consciousness. He is totally in the present, in the moment.

The brothers agree. Collette is his to marry. The brothers tell the sister. Fortunately, it brings her joy. Jacques is one of the "family."

Chapter 30

It's early morning at the Airfield in Montreal. Jacques, dressed in flying gear and goggles is standing next to another man, also dressed in flying gear and goggles who wears a shirt that reads "Flight Instructor." Jacques climbs into the cockpit, and the Instructor sits beside hm. Jacques revs up the engine, pulls back the stick, and the plane goes up.

Jacques dips and soars, laughing. He loves the exquisite power it gives him to fly the plane. It has been his dream most of his life, even as a kid on the farm, looking up at the sky. He says to the Instructor, "This ought to do it. I have enough hours now for my Pilot's license."

The Instructor replies, "From now on, it's all yours. You are one cool customer. I would fly with you anytime."

Jacques brings the plane into the landing, and he and the Instructor deplane. Jacques takes off his helmet and goggles as they head for the hangar. "I can't wait to get out into the bush. The first thing I'm doing is moose hunting. I grew up shooting pheasants. Now it's time for something bigger."

Jacques shakes hands with his Instructor and walks off the field. He approaches a black limousine parked at the curb. The driver salutes Jacques and opens the door for him. He gets into the limo, and they drive off, passing down the road from the airfield, through downtown Montreal, to the large circular drive in front of Jacques' mansion in Mount Royal.

The ride gives Jacques time to look back over the past few years.

He feels triumphant about his progress. In the short time he has been in Montreal, he has totally turned his life around and moved into the mainstream. He owns the Blue Bonnet, he is accepted into the DuBois clan, he is married to Collette, a gorgeous woman with a pleasant personality whose company he enjoys. For him it isn't exactly love, but he has no intention of getting carried off by emotion. That hasn't worked for him. He is attracted enough to her that he enjoys his time in bed with her. They have no children. She is sorry. Jacques has no regrets. He has had more than enough of those.

The blended "family" has meant a blended "business," and he has made the transition with Hungarian Joe and Frenchie out of the day-to-day operation of the track. They stop in to make sure things are running smoothly, but they have shifted much of the gambling business over to their own space next to the Carat Club. He lets Hungarian Joe and Frenchie run that. He has grown into the role of the overseer. The brothers manage the Carat Club, Joe and Frenchie manage the gambling, and he has a manager to oversee the operation of the track. He just makes sure each one is doing the job well. That's pretty amazing given the short time he's been in the "family."

He has the insurance policies. He's the beneficiary on every one of them: Collette, her mother, the brothers, Hungarian Joe, Frenchie, the three sellers of the Blue Bonnet, Catherine, Joseph. The sellers of the Blue Bonnet know, but the others do not. He pays for the policies. It's as close as he can get to a "sure" thing.

It's very important for him to have a "sure thing." He waited for years before he contacted Catherine and Joseph. He wanted to be sure they had stopped looking for him. He didn't go direct. He went through his cousin Leo, the one who owns the car dealership in Windsor. He's a successful business man in Windsor. He and Jacques grew up together. Jacques doesn't exactly trust him, either, except he owes him money. That makes Leo accountable.

It worked out ok getting back in touch with Joseph and Catherine. They were relieved he was alive. They are running his farm, what he had expected. They still see Francine and Elsie. They come and visit the farm. Catherine and Joseph send food home with them from the farm and the slaughter house. When Jacques disappeared, Catherine and Joseph paid the child support. They always liked Francine. Vincent comes to the farm. The other boys do not. Jacques always had his doubts about the other boys. Shannon has remarried. It doesn't feel messy anymore.

His big regret is Vincent. Catherine and Joseph have told him about how he's earning butcher's wages, that he bought his own car, that he comes and helps on the farm, that he's a good hunter, that he's paying his own tuition in a private school, that he looks and acts a lot like Jacques. They even sent him a picture.

When he discussed with Hungarian Joe and Frenchie that he wanted to bring Vincent to Montreal, they suggested his Cousin Leo should talk to him. Jacques thought he had made him an offer he couldn't refuse: $10,000 in cash, live with him and Collette in Montreal, his education paid for.

It turned out it wasn't a pleasant meeting. Leo had asked Vincent to stop by on his way to the farm. So he did. He drove up in his own car to

Leo's Ford dealership. It's hard to know what Leo said or how he said it, but Vincent said "no." He asked if it included his brothers. That surprised Jacques, perhaps because he was an only child and always thought only about himself. Leo wasn't prepared for that question.

But Leo wasn't prepared, either, when Vincent said, "All of my life, ever since I watched my father beat my mother, I have wanted to kill him. That's why I have practiced shooting. And now, after all these years, he wants me to come and live with him. No way!"

Jacques knows everything is negotiable. He should have figured out how to do it himself. He shouldn't have left it to Leo. He shouldn't have put something so important to him in the hands of other people: Hungarian Joe, Frenchie, Leo. But it had been tricky since Collette and the "family" didn't know about his past, about Shannon and the boys. He wasn't sure how he would have introduced Vincent if he had agreed to come. Maybe he was saved. Well, that was over, at least for the time being.

The limo stops by the front door. The driver gets out and opens the door for Jacques. Jacques goes up the front steps and opens the front door, carrying his helmet as he enters. He puts the helmet down on the vestibule table. He sees Collette, his wife, a tall, voluptuous brunette with hair carefully elevated into an elegant bun, with tiny tendrils cascading down the temples. Everything about her is perfectly finished – her red sheath dress that clings to her good figure, her high heels, her way of walking, presenting herself.

She holds out her hands for a hug. They embrace. She says, "So Jacques, are you now a pilot?"

"I am officially now a pilot. The paper work is all filled out, and I can get my license. This morning was the last hour. And I have already found a plane to buy."

Collette gives him a high five. "You came in just in time. I am leaving to have lunch with Mama."

Jacques says, "Give her my love. You take the limo. I'm having dinner tonight with your brothers at the Club. As soon as I take a shower, I'll drive myself. Don't expect me to be home until late." He kisses her on the cheek.

Chapter 31

Vincent has been making friends at St. Patrick's. He is probably the only student in the school paying his own tuition. The others come from affluent Catholic families willing to pay the extra money to give their children the fine scholastic training offered at St. Patrick's, along with the religious education that comes with it. Vincent's job as a butcher gives him enough for tuition, car payments, gas, and a little to spare. He has the prestige of owning a Chrysler Imperial, far better car than the head priest is driving. The priest even asked him, "Your father's car?" And Vincent said, "No, it's my car. I'm a butcher." The priest replied, "It makes my car look like a piece of junk."

One of his good friends is Danny Riley. They are both Irish, and they both love to hunt and shoot. In fact, Danny is preparing for the Olympic Marksman competition. One Friday afternoon, just as they are getting out of school. Danny stops Vincent in the parking lot: "Say, Vince, my Dad is taking me down to Camp Perry to the firing range tomorrow. It's his day off from the Dearborn Police Department. Want to come?"

Vincent usually works on Saturdays at Stein and Stein, but he actually had the next day off. He'd planned to drive to Canada to the farm, but this was an opportunity he couldn't pass up. He said, "If I can get to shoot, too, I'd like to come." Danny said, "My Dad can set that up. He knows all of the guys."

So early Saturday morning, Vincent and Danny are sitting beside

Ben Riley in the front seat of his truck. Vincent says, "Where are we going? I never heard of Camp Perry."

Ben fills him in. "Camp Perry is in Ohio on the shores of Lake Erie. This is where Vincent fishes. It is named for Commodore Perry, the American Commander who defeated the British in the Battle of Lake Erie in the War of 1812. It's near Port Clinton, Ohio." Vincent knows about the War of 1812. Catherine's Indian tribe in Canada, the Senecas, fought on the side of the British in that war. They succeeded in taking Fort Detroit.

Camp Perry is amazing. It has the largest and best equipped rifle and pistol ranges in the United States, with four major ranges that provide 210 rifle and 20 revolver targets that can be operated simultaneously from 200, 600, and 800 yard ranges. Vincent is in awe. He has never seen anything like it.

Danny is at the 200 yard rifle range. He is shooting a .22 rifle. He demonstrates to Vincent the three positions for shooting: lying down, kneeling, standing. Vincent watches attentively. When he hunts, he is always standing. A young Oriental man is firing next to Danny. The Olympian trainees are all up and down the range, and the Coach walks the line, observing. He will be choosing the members of the team. Vincent is impressed with Danny's accuracy. He is dying to get a chance.

Finally, Danny says, "Here, Vincent, I'm going to get a hamburger. Take my place and shoot. I promised you would get a turn."

Vincent takes the rifle and practices, first lying down then kneeling, then standing up. The Coach stops and watches him. He says to Vincent, "Why don't you shoot with the guy standing next to you, just for practice."

Vincent says, "Sure, that would be great." They begin taking turns. Vincent shoots, then the Oriental shoots. Vincent shoots, then the Oriental shoots. Vincent hits the target every time. He does better than the other guy.

The Coach says, "Do you know who that guy is? He's the National Champion of China. If you can beat him, you have a good chance of making the team."

Vincent says, "I'm just shooting my friend's gun while he's getting something to eat."

The Coach asks, "How long have you been shooting? You're a real pro."

Vincent replies, "Since I was 9. My grandfather gave me a gun, and I hunt on his farm."

The Coach says, "I sure wish I had you on my team."

Vincent knows from watching Danny that he could probably outshoot him. He never thought about shooting as a sport. For him it was a necessity, shooting to kill his father. It has been on his mind off and on ever since his mother's beating. It came back to him clearly when his Uncle Leo asked him to stop by his Ford dealership in Windsor.

He wasn't prepared for the proposition. He hasn't seen Jacques since they fled to Detroit. He knew he had a farm next to his grandparents, but he never went near it. He had heard from a cousin that Jacques wasn't living at the farm anymore, but he didn't know where he went. Whenever Jacques' name had been mentioned to him, he changed the subject. It always stirred up the same emotions of hatred and revenge that he felt as a child, a rage so immense that it totally overwhelmed his reason, a rage that frightened him a little because he had no control over it. It just came and immersed his entire being.

So when his Uncle Leo explained that Jacques was living in Montreal, was engaged in business there, very successful, remarried, a friend of the Prime Minister, Vincent heard him but didn't hear him. And when he said his father was offering him $10,000 if he would move to Montreal and live with him, that he would pay for his College education, Vincent heard him, but didn't hear him. The words didn't penetrate the rage he was feeling.

When Vincent asked, "What about my brothers?" his uncle replied, "Your father only wants you."

Had Vincent been rational, he might have said, "Let me think about it." He might have remembered that he liked to ride in the truck with Jacques, that he liked to hunt with Jacques. He might have remembered being in the slaughter house with him when the lightening struck. But then he might also have remembered when Jacques fed the two men to the hogs.

Had Vincent been rational, he might have considered what a fortune $10,000 represented. You could buy a house in Detroit with $10,000. His Uncle told him his father lived in a mansion. Vincent's mother and stepfather lived in a little two-bedroom house. He and his brothers shared one room. His stepfather worked for the gas company. His mother had left the B24 factory and now worked at J.L. Hudson. They would never in their life be able to save $10,000, let alone give that to him.

Had Vincent been rational, he might have considered what an extraordinary gift it would have been to have his education paid for. He could be like the other students at St. Patrick's with parents footing the bill. He could engage in marksmanship as a sport rather than an expression of his rage, a rich man's sport.

Had Vincent been rational, he might have said that he would like to meet his father and talk about it. That never occurred to him. He immediately said, "No. Absolutely not! I won't even consider it. I hate my father."

He got in his car and drove away from the Ford dealership on to McGregor and his grandparents' farm. He told Shannon about it. Then he put it out of his mind. Shannon, of course, was indignant Jacques only wanted Vincent, not his brothers.

Chapter 32

Jacques pulls up to the front of the Carat Club in a 1954 black Cadillac. A doorman and a valet stand by the awning-covered front entrance. The valet opens the door on the driver's side, and Jacques gets out of the car. Jacques is dressed in a black suit, white shirt, and blue tie. He shakes hands with the valet, and moves toward the entrance. The doorman greets him, and Jacques pauses to shake his hand. The doorman opens the door as the valet pulls away from the curb. This gives us a chance to see the environment this butcher and farmer from McGregor has mastered and even conquered in his new home in Montreal.

Jacques enters the foyer of the Club and scans the entrance. Two attractive women in low-cut dresses stand behind the front desk. Behind them are a series of three double doors, each one opening into a separate area of the Club. A doorman stands beside each of the double doors. Jacques greets the women and walks to the double doors in the middle.

Jacques looks in upon the bar and dining room with a stage at the far end. It is late afternoon, and only two men sit at the bar on the right side of the room. The stage is dark, and bus boys are busy setting the tables. Only a few tables are occupied, and the waitresses, dressed in low-cut leotards revealing their breasts, stand in mesh stockings and high heels near the bar, joking with the bartender. A series of private doors are lined up on the left side of the room. This is where Jacques will be joining his brothers-in-law for dinner in a couple of hours.

Jacques goes to the door, opens it and passes through. The

doorman tips his hat as he leaves. Jacques turns to his left to enter a second double door. The doorman tips his hat and opens to door for him. Jacques looks in at a large room. Hungarian Joe stands behind a desk on the far side. Bookies are seated in a row behind him, along the back of the desk. Hungarian Joe waves to Jacques.

Frenchie stands in front of a wall-size blackboard at the end of the room, talking on the phone and writing the results on the blackboard. Men mill around the room. On the right side of the room, a cashier in a cage hands out cash. Friday afternoon pay stubs litter the floor. The race track is thriving, and so is their additional gambling business. Jacques has managed to concentrate everything in one place. He waves to Frenchie and turns to leave the room.

Jacques leaves the room, nods to the doorman, and crosses over to the double doors on his right, those just behind the front desk. The doorman tips his hat and opens the door. Jacques looks in at a long hallway with a waiting room at the end. A receptionist sits behind a desk on the right hand side. Jacques greets the receptionist:

"Well, Rosie, ready for the weekend?"

"Yes, sir, my brother's getting married."

Jacques says, "Give him and the bride my good wishes. Why don't you go on home for the weekend to get ready." He turns to his left and opens a door to a private office. An attractive woman dressed in a business suit sits at the front desk.

Jacques says, "Well, Sonia, I am officially a pilot."

She replies, "Congratulations! The salesman for the plane called this morning. I told him you would probably want to meet with him tomorrow to finalize the sale. Your brother-in-law called. They will be here for dinner at 7:00."

Jacques says, "Thanks, Sonia. I need to make a few phone calls before they get here, and I'll call the salesman, too. You can go on home. Have a good weekend."

He walks past her and opens a large door leading into an inner office. A huge mahogany desk with leather chairs in front of it flanks the left side of the room. A conference table with six chairs dominates the middle if the room. A bar stretches along the right side of the room. Jacques takes off his jacket, hangs it on his chair, sits behind the desk and picks up the phone. What a day!

Just at 6:55 Jacques hangs up the phone, looks at his watch, and puts his jacket back on. It's time for dinner. He goes out the door of his private office, down the hall to the double door, and opens it. The doorman tips his hat. The middle double doors are now wide open. People are stopping at the front desk, checking in, paying the "cover" charge" and being escorted inside. Friday nights are big at the Carat Club.

Jacques looks inside, takes in the room, and sees his brother-in-laws sitting at a table near the front of the room. Strippers are dancing on the stage, and the room is humming with laughter and conversation. Almost every table is either taken or marked "Reserve." Jacques goes to the table and shakes hands with Jimmy and Freddie Dubois who stand to greet him.

Jimmy says, "Business is booming! It's improved since you joined the family. Collette married the right man."

Jacques laughs. He notices they have already ordered his favorite drink and had it waiting for him, Canadian Club on the rocks. Freddie tells the waitress they are having a meeting and to come back in an hour to take their orders. Jacques tells them he got his pilot's license and tomorrow he will buy a plane. They congratulate him.

It was always his dream, to be a pilot. He used to look up at the geese on the farm flying overhead, and wonder what it would be like to be looking down from up there. Now he is "up there." They've done well for themselves, he, Hungarian Joe, and Frenchie. Or actually, he has done well for Hungarian Joe and Frenchie.

He needs people he can trust, people who can run the bookie business and not steal him blind. He needs people who know his roots who will cover for him if he needs to embellish his story. He needs people dependent upon him so they won't be tempted to rat on him, or set him up, or attempt to go into business for themselves.

He likes these brothers-in-law, but he knows them for what they are. They are the powerful DuBois. They let him in "by marriage." He's good for the family. They took a cut from the race-track in exchange for a cut they gave him in the Carat Club. They are in business together. But Jacques knows he walks the line with them. They can give the order at any time and wipe him out. He doesn't dwell on it. He knows he is smarter than they are, otherwise he wouldn't have made it "in." "In" and "out" are two sides of the same coin. He never forgets it.

And some of this business he finds unsavory. Booze and betting are pretty straight. The prostitution bothers him, maybe going back to the game in McGregor and the little girl being raised by the mother's husband. Not that he feels guilt. It was all part of the game, for him and for Shannon.

The strippers have finished the first set. The women come down from the stage and walk provocatively through the dining room. Couples are disappearing through the doors on the side of the room marked A, B, C, D, E. This is the big money, not the bar, not the food, not the entertainment on the stage. It's all a cover: The "Cover Charge."

Chapter 33

From the moment Vincent had his own paper route for *The Detroit Times*, he has been paying his tuition for his Catholic schools. He actually felt older than Shannon and responsible when they moved to Detroit, like he was the cause. Shannon has remarried, an Italian World War II Navy veteran she met at the factory. Vincent went for a full year, living in the house with them, before he would speak to his step-father. He didn't know who he hated more: his father or his father's substitute

Every Sunday Gino and Shannon would fight. Every Sunday they would make up. Every Sunday Gino would cook dinner. He was a great cook, the best spaghetti and meatballs in the world. Shannon was Irish. Everything she cooked tasted like smelly shoes in a canvas bag. Finally, after eleven months, Gino said to Vincent, "I am really tired of not talking." Eureka! Vincent had won. The first one to talk loses.

Gino has a job now with the gas company. He checks meters, sometimes goes on repair calls. Shannon has a job at the J. L. Hudson company, housewares. They make enough to have their own two-bedroom house and to provide food for the family, but that is all, the same hand to mouth existence of everyone they know.

So Vincent has been finding his way. One of his customers on his paper route is a man from Tennessee, Mr. Baggett. Mr. Baggett, who plays six different string instruments and can perform non-stop with blue grass music from home, is an avid hunter. Vincent told him about hunting on his grandfather's farm. One day Mr. Baggett said, "The neighbor next door has a shotgun for sale for $20. Do you want to buy it?" Vincent did. The shells came with it. So now he has guns on both side of the Bridge

Vincent has been accepted at St. Patrick's High School. St. Patrick's is in Wyandotte, downriver, named after the Native American tribe known as the Wyandot, part of the Huron nation. It was near here that Pontiac plotted his failed attack against the British garrisoned at Fort Detroit in1763. They were a farming tribe relying heavily on hunting, fishing and trading .Their main mode of transportation was by birch bark canoe. In 1818, the Wyandot signed a treaty with the U.S. government, relinquishing this land. Some moved to an area near Flat Rock, Michigan, amazingly enough, Vincent's favorite place to hunt pheasant when he is not at the farm in Canada.

Wyandotte is upscale from Lincoln Park where Vincent and his mother and grandparents live. Vincent is an outsider, paying his own tuition, driving himself to school. Admission to St. Patrick's High School is by application only, and they only accept 80 students in each class from all of the Detroit area. Vincent's record in elementary school has gained his admission, along with his ability to pay.

Vincent's reputation at St. Patrick's is growing. He immediately distinguished himself in his freshman class when they went through their hazing. The seniors all formed a line, and the freshmen were required to move down the line getting paddled by the seniors. Vincent responded by fighting back, hitting the first one in the nose, then the second one. He was only part way down the line before the seniors decided to leave him alone. After that, no one has   messed with him.

The story of the sacks of crows spread all over the school. The girls went home and told their parents about the horrible boy who brought them crows to dissect and how obnoxious it was to have to cut through the feathers and into the crows. The boys went home and told their parents how great it was that one of their classmates brought them crows to dissect, how exciting it was to look inside and see what was there. The nuns at the school all talk about him, how resourceful he is, how dependable.

Dan and Ben Riley came back from Fort Perry, and the story of Vincent's shooting there spread. Up to that point, Vincent had really not begun to "mix" with the other kids, and they didn't know anything about him, just that he came from Lincoln Park and drove his own car to school. Danny praised his shooting, told them how he had beat the Olympic champion from China: standing, kneeling, and lying on the ground.

Vincent is on the football team, left end, and St. Patrick's has been winning. He has developed notoriety there. When they played across town, at Mt. Carmel, Vincent went across the field and told his buddy from grade school that St. Patrick's would "kick their ass." He laughed and joked with their entire team. Then he came back across the field to St. Patrick's side, and St. Patrick's did "kick their ass."

Now October 20th has arrived, and Vincent picks up his riders to school instead of having them meet him. Each one places a shotgun in the trunk of the car. Then he drives into the school parking lot. Father Martin is standing nearby when he parks. Father Martin polices the parking lot and keeps roll for the school. Vincent says, "Well, Father Martin, we won't be in school today. We're on our way to Flat Rock."

Father Martin asks, "Why not?" Vincent says, "It's the first day of Pheasant Season. It starts at 10:00 a.m." He opens the trunk, and Father Martin sees the shotguns.

Father Martin says, "Bring me a couple, and I won't mark you absent."

They arrive in Flat Rock. Vincent's Gordon Setter in Canada, Jake, fathered a puppy, and it is with Vincent in the car. Vincent wants to break him in. The other boys make jokes about the puppy being useless, and they set off for the cornfield. Vincent holds back, waiting to see what the puppy will do. He knows the importance of hunting birds with a good bird dog. This puppy comes from a noble father with a great record.

The puppy zeroes in on the farrow, just beyond the car. It starts down the farrow. Vincent thinks, "Well, that's strange, but I've got all day." The puppy wags its tail, its head down. They go in about 100 feet, and a cock pheasant flies up from the bottom of the farrow. Vincent waits until it is totally air-bound: aims, fires, and brings him down.

The puppy has stirred up more birds. Who would have thought they would be so close to the ground. Another one flies up. Vincent waits, watches, aims, shoots. He is careful to avoid the hens. He knows the laws. Bird after bird flies up. Each time Vincent waits, aims, shoots.

Vincent has hardly moved. In a couple of hours, he and the puppy, now having earned the name "Sharp," have collected a pile of cock birds. Sharp not only instinctively knows how to stir them up. He knows how to go in, fetch, and bring them back. The puppy is wagging his tail, so proud of himself, so pleased that Vincent pets him, thanks him.

The other boys have had mixed luck in their cornfield. They have two cocks. The sun is starting to move down, and they decide to go back and find Vincent. They see him standing by the car with Sharp and his pile of cocks. Their quota is two apiece, and thanks to Vincent, they've made the limit. They flip coins to see who has to give up one apiece for Father Martin.

They pet Sharp and apologize to Vincent for being critical. They also apologize to Sharp. Paul says, "Do you know who you are, Vincent? You are Wyatt Earp."

After that Vincent in known at St. Patrick's as Wyatt Earp.

Chapter 34

In the meantime, Hungarian Joe, and Frenchie are sitting in the passenger seats in Jacques' pontoon bi-plane. It is early morning. They are all dressed in hunting clothes with hunting gear and guns stacked behind them in the back of the plane. The plane is traveling northeast from Quebec, toward Newfoundland. In Western Newfoundland the aircraft climbs as it crosses over the Long Range Mountains. Jacques adeptly lands the plane on its pontoons on Deer Lake.

Jacques says, "I could easily have made a career as a bush pilot. Nothing gives me more pleasure than getting out in the wild in this plane."

Frenchie replies, "You're a natural. I never feel afraid when you fly the plane. Great October weather."

Hungarian Joe pipes in, "Better yet, they guarantee we all get a moose."

Jacques steers the plane up to the shore, parks it near a large wooden log lodge, off to the side. The three men get out of the plane and start removing their gear. They put their duffel bags over their shoulders, grab their guns, and set off for the Lodge. As they enter the Lodge, they see men in hunting clothes sitting at the table in the main part of the cabin, eating breakfast or drinking coffee. The boasts are going all around.

"That bull had 16 points. I'm shipping the cape, antlers and meat back tomorrow. What a week!"

"We never saw so many moose. The guides have been great. I got mine the first day."

The three men take in all their chatter and boasting, set down their gear, and walk to the front desk. The man behind the desk comes out to greet them, shakes their hands, and directs them to the room where they will be sleeping. He tells them they are still having breakfast. Jacques asks, "Will we be able to go out today?"

The clerk replies, "Sure thing. Your guide will be here in an hour. You will have a full afternoon."

By early afternoon, the three men are following their guide into the Newfoundland bog with pine trees, burned stumps, berry bushes. The trees have turned red and yellow, and the scenery and smell are spectacular.

The guide says, "We hunt here in the open. We stay in one spot and wait for the moose to come to us. I'll call them. We get them within 200 feet of you before you need to shoot or stalk."

Jacques says, "We're ready." He is holding his 30.06 rifle, expectant.

The moose call reverberates through the air. The three men, stationed with guns ready, look out over the bog. From a far corner, a bull moose, 1500 pounds with huge rack, approaches from the right toward Jacques. He lifts his gun, aims, waits. The bull keeps coming. Jacques stays perfectly still.

The guide instructs: "Don't hurry. Let him come. He's downwind from us and doesn't know we're here."

The moose approaches. It passes through burned stumps and brush pine trees, oblivious he is being watched. As he moves into the clearing, Jacques fires. The moose goes down. Then it gets back up, lurching forward, then halting. He is wounded. Jacques moves closer to the moose, stalks him. He lifts his gun, aims carefully, shoots again, this time hitting the moose in the neck. The moose goes down.

The four men approach the fallen moose. The guide pulls out a tape and measures the antlers. "20 inches. Big fella!" He counts the points of the antlers. "16 points. That will look great on the wall. Not bad for your first afternoon. Let's get the pictures before the sun goes down"

Jacques poses next to the moose, holding his rifle. The sun sinks lower in the sky. The men shiver as the air becomes cooler. Frenchie says, "Time to drink."

The next morning they are out early. When they reach within 100 yards of the clearing, next to the pond, four moose have gathered. Frenchie says, "You shoot, Jacques. You're better than Joe and me." Jacques lifts his 30.06, aims carefully, and shoots. He hits the nearest moose, and it goes down in the water. The other three turn to flee. Jacques fires again. A second moose goes down.

Hungarian Joe and Frenchie both fire at the departing moose, but neither of their bullets hit the target. The four men advance toward the two fallen moose. The first one gets up, lurches forward. Jacques fires again. The moose goes down. The guide measures the antlers on the first one: "16 inches." He goes to the second moose and measures: "18 inches. Good work! Let's get your pictures."

The men each pose separately beside a moose, kneeling down with their guns on display. The guide beckons to two men nearby, Lodge employees. He says, "Come on over here and give us a hand dressing these out. Boy, oh boy, what a morning!" He attaches tags to each animal and comments, "No guesswork here about who's the best shot."

Hungarian Joe says, "God damn. We came along for the ride, the grub, and the booze. In two days, we got our quota. Now what?"

Jacques says, "We're here for the week. No one expects us back."

The guide says, "You've got that pontoon plane. The fishing in the big lake just north of here is great for Northerns and Walleye. We have boats there. We can set it up. You can fish during the day and come back to the Lodge at night."

The next morning, Jacques glides the pontoon plane to the landing on Eagle Lake. It is a remote area, with the large, very blue pristine lake surrounded by pine trees. A loon circles overhead. There is a beaver house near the shore, and the beavers swim and flap their tales. A man greets them as they depart the plane. The Lodge has arranged for a guide and a boat, and he leads them to it, just big enough for the four of them. It is totally equipped with fishing gear and bait, and all they have to do is get in and start fishing. The three of them have lines in the water, and the guide holds a net.

Jacques is the first to get a tug, actually more than a tug. He pulls in the fish and the guide lowers the net. When he takes the fish out of the net and puts it alongside the ruler fastened to the side of the boat, it measures 28 inches, a Walleye.

The guide says, "You're off to a good start."

The men fish all day, and when they finally pull back up to shore, they have a stringer of fish. The guide says, "All of you line up and have your picture taken." They spread the stringer among themselves, beaming. They are returning to the Lodge, and the guide assists them in loading the fish in the plane. They have been promised their catch will be their dinner.

That night they sit at a picnic table in the Lodge dining room in front of the fire, boasting and laughing. Plates heaped with fried fish anchor the middle of the table, surrounded by steins of beer, glasses of whiskey, mounds of mashed potatoes. A perfect end to the first half week of an amazing adventure. They have four more days!

Chapter 35

The yard of the Joseph and Catherine's farmhouse in McGregor is full of cars, all the way down to the road. A bush plane with pontoons is parked in the barnyard. All of the porch and yard lights are lighted up, and the house has an unusual vitality. The lilacs near the door are in bloom. Looking in from outside, you can see people milling around.

Inside, a party atmosphere prevails. The house is full of people, all dressed up, with men in suits and women in fancy dresses, an unusual scene for McGregor. They are laughing, moving around the parlor, drinking wine and whiskey. Catherine, for once, isn't wearing an apron, isn't even in the kitchen. A bar tender is pouring the drinks, and young women are carrying platters of food to the dining room table.

Jacques moves around the room, greeting the guests. It is the first time in years that he has been back to McGregor. When he escaped to Montreal, wearing the butcher coat, he cut off all communication. While the heat was on, after the diamond heist, while they were looking for him, Catherine and Joseph could not know where he went, what he was doing.

The loose diamonds could not be traced. He sold them, one at a time, to different jewelers and merchants, sometimes sending Frenchie or Hungarian Joe to make the sale. Montreal was big enough for discretion, and he came into town quietly. For months he was in a learning mode, observing people and patterns, groups, getting a feel for how things worked, who was pulling the strings. His affable manner made him acceptable, and he didn't assert himself. He could shift easily between French and English, and he quickly discerned that the Italian and the Irish were more ingrown and impenetrable by an outsider.

It was three years before he made the phone call to Joseph and Catherine. Even then he did not give them an address or a phone number. He just wanted them to know he was alive and well. They reported to him on Vincent, who came frequently to the farm. They were in touch with Francine and had picked up the child support when he left. Joseph was farming both farms.

Jacques was the extreme example of escape, but it was a common pattern of behavior with farmers like Joseph who ruled with an iron hand and who expected the son to obey, to become the farmer he was, to assume the role of the father. The only way the son could escape was to run away. Sometime they never came back. Sometimes they came home and became the farmer the father expected. Catherine and Joseph just continued on, accepting the anxiety and the despair, and hoping that some day their only son would return to them.

This is a glorious event for them. Jacques is so well dressed, so self-assured. He flew into McGregor in his own plane. They can present him to family and friends with pride. For years they had not even uttered his name to anyone, closing out the family issue that caused them so much pain, pushing away their emotions with work, the ceaseless rhythm of planting, growing, weeding, harvesting, the daily chores of feeding the livestock and poultry, the butchering, the selling. Only the cold and dark months of November through February brought any rest from the daily routine, and even then they didn't talk about it, not even between themselves.

And tonight for the first time, Jacques and Vincent will be together. It is a dream of Catherine and Joseph, for their son and their favorite grandson to be together with them in the same room. They don't know why he isn't there yet. Vincent is so dependable, so punctual, so respectful. Jacques keeps going to the window, watching.

The dining room table is finally filled with food, a feast typical of Joseph and Catherine: ham, turkey, mashed potatoes, gravy, devilled eggs, green beans, macaroni and cheese. A wedding cake anchors the middle of the table. Jacques has been circulating among the guests, talking, laughing, every few minutes going to the window and looking out. Catherine approaches him. They can't wait any longer.

"The food is ready. It will grow cold. It's time to eat."

Two young girls are circulating among the guests, passing out glasses of champagne. Jacques goes to the center of the room and taps his glass.

"I propose a toast. To Catherine and Joseph: Fifty years of marriage, fifty years of hard labor and good results, fifty years of service to the town and the church, to family and friends."

The guests cheer: "Hear! Hear! Hear! Hear!" They all clink glasses.

Catherine wipes tears from her eyes. Joseph steps forward to speak: "Thank you for coming. It means so much to us to have you here. It means so much for Jacques to be here with us. The only one missing is Vincent. He said he was coming. Anyway, let's eat."

The guests all line up, fill their plates, find places around the room to sit and eat. Jacques walks to the window and looks out again, peering into the darkness. It is as if he is alone in the room full of people.

Vincent, 18, drives up to the farmhouse in his blue Chrysler. He observes the large number of cars in the yard and the plane. He's late. He's always on time. His grandparents expected him two hours ago, but he had to work late. The blond with big boobs and long hair sits beside him in the front seat.

Vincent says to her "We must be the last ones here. I didn't intend to be so late. On top of staying at work, we had the delay on the Bridge. I don't want to disappoint my grandparents on their 50th Anniversary."

He parks the car, gets out, opens the door for the girl. They walk up to the front porch of the house. He sees his Uncle Leo standing by the front door. He has just opened the door when his Uncle nudges him away. "I don't think you want to go in there. Your father is here for your Grandparents' Anniversary party."

Vincent says, "Thanks for telling me. I'm out of here."

He feels welling up inside of him the hatred and resentment that he has carried all of his life, ever since he watched Jacques beat his mother, break her feet, ever since they escaped to Detroit. The intention he has carried with him, to kill his father, is as strong as ever. He cannot take it into the party, to disrupt the special event.

Vincent takes the arm of the girl, leads her off of the porch, opens the passenger door of the blue Chrysler, and pushes her inside.

The girl says, "I thought we came here for a party."

Vincent replies, "We did. But I've changed my mind. We're going back to Detroit."

Vincent gets back in to his car and starts the motor. Jacques stands in the window, looking out. He sees Vincent getting back into his car. He begins to cry.

PART 3

Chapter 36

Vincent, late 20's, and Anthony, one year younger, are standing before the screen in the Toronto airport checking flight times. Vincent is wearing a black suit, white shirt and tie. Anthony is more casually dressed in a sport shirt and slacks. It is July and warm in Canada. Vincent points to a flight on the screen:

"That's the one we want to Montreal."

The two brothers walk toward the gate. The plane is boarding, and the attendant takes their boarding passes. They start down the aisle toward their seats. Vincent looks up, astonished to see Catherine and Joseph on the same flight. They are both wearing black.

Joseph says, "We didn't expect you boys to get here yet."

Vincent says, "We had good connecting flights from LA and caught a room last night. Frank will get in tomorrow from Germany."

Catherine says, "The man who called us will meet us in Montreal. We can all go together."

Vincent and Anthony go to their seats. Vincent has the window seat. As they fasten their seat belts, the Captain's voice comes over the loudspeaker: "The flight will be 45 minutes. We should arrive in Montreal on time. The temperature in Montreal is 22 Celsius, 70 Fahrenheit."

Vincent is looking out the window as the flight lands. A large group of people are waiting on the ground. Vincent spots a tall man in a black suit, black hat, and black moustache in the crowd. He points to him.

"There, Anthony, that looks like our old man's friend."

Catherine and Joseph are descending the stairs, followed by Vincent and Anthony. The man in the black suit approaches Joseph and Catherine, the oldest people on the flight. He shakes their hands and introduces himself:

"I am Henri, your son's friend and business partner. I am so sorry for the loss of your son."

Joseph replies, "Thank you."

Vincent and Anthony come alongside their grandparents. Henri acknowledges them and asks, "And who is with you?"

Vincent puts out his hand: "I am the oldest son, Vincent. This is my brother, Anthony"

Henri, visibly shocked by Vincent's admission as the oldest son, kisses Vincent on both cheeks, then turns to Anthony to shake his hand. Henri says, "I will need to make a phone call before we leave. Please excuse me."

Vincent says, "We have rented a car. We need to get our luggage and pick it up. Will we be able to follow you?

Henri replies, "Of course."

Vincent, Anthony, and Joseph go to the baggage claim and Catherine takes a seat along the wall. Henri is speaking on the pay phone in the corner. He looks furtively at Vincent as he speaks. Vincent takes both of his grandparents' suitcases, and Anthony takes the suitcases of the two brothers. Vincent goes to where Catherine is sitting and puts their suitcases beside her. Then he and Anthony head for the car rentals, toward the sign reading: *Voiture de Location*. Joseph and Catherine wait for Henri to get off the phone.

At Henri's direction, Catherine and Joseph stand at the curb with their suitcases. Henri drives up in a black car, gets out, opens the trunk and loads their suitcases. He opens the back door of the car for Catherine, and she gets in. Joseph opens the front passenger door and gets in the front seat. Vincent and Anthony drive up behind Henri's car in their white rental Ford, Vincent driving. Henri beckons to them.

"We will go directly to the mortuary in Saint Jovite. They are expecting you. Follow me."

The two cars pull out of the airport. They go down the surface street to the highway. The road sign reads: "MONT TREMBLANT – 130 KM."

Vincent says, "We might as well enjoy the scenery." The road winds through the mountains, passing rugged terrain.

The two cars pass a sign, "SAINT JOVITE" and Henri leads them down a side road, through the village, past shops and a post office.

They stop in front of the mortuary. The sign in front reads "MORTUAIRE SAINT JOVITE."

Vincent parks the white Ford, and he and Anthony walk forward to Henri's parked car. Vincent opens the back door of Henri's car for Catherine and takes her hand. Joseph opens his door and gets out. Vincent, Anthony, Joseph and Catherine follow Henri into the mortuary.

People are clustered in distinct groups in the room. On the left side, near the open coffin, a group of 20 men are gathered all in black suits. Henri goes to them, introduces the family. They stare at Vincent, visibly shaken. Henri leads them to the coffin.

Jacques is laid out, wearing a black suit, white shirt, tie and matching handkerchief. Vincent looks just like the corpse. This is the first time he has seen his father since he left McGregor at the age of 5. He is startled by the resemblance. No one has ever commented about it to him. He looks away, however, unmoved. Catherine begins to weep. Joseph passes out, a huge crash as he reaches the floor. Vincent attends to him. Joseph recovers, rests in a chair.

Another group is gathered on the right side of the room. A beautiful young woman with black hair and green eyes holds a one-year old child on her hip. Another boy, approximately two years old, clings to her ankles. She is surrounded by a man and woman, probably in their early 50's, and several younger men and women. The family resemblance is strong, all with black hair and black eyes. Only the young woman has green eyes. Henri leaves his group and takes

Jacques' family to them for introduction. The vibration is hostile.

Henri says to Joseph and Catherine, "This is your son's wife and their two boys. She is a Mohawk. Her name is Latonya,"

Vincent goes to the woman. She looks at him as if she knows him, and she begins to cry. The family moves aside as Vincent shakes her hand and touches the boys affectionately.

Vincent says to her, "I am the oldest son. I am sorry for your loss. I am here with my father's parents and my brother. We were called and asked to come."

She replies, "Thank you for coming. We were told to expect you. You must come to the house. We are ready for you."

Chapter 37

Catherine and Joseph have been standing aside. Vincent takes Latonya by the arm and leads her over to them. It is a strange and awkward moment for them. They knew nothing about this woman, nothing about this life. After their 50th Anniversary, Jacques would occasionally fly in for a visit and then leave. He never really talked about his business or his life, even where he lived. He would talk with them about the farm, about the people in McGregor, about the family burial plot they had established. He would eat heartily, praise Catherine for her food, and he would leave.

So here is this strange woman, approximately the same age as Vincent. This is their son's "widow." They shake her hand.

Latonya says, "We have been expecting you, and we want you to stay with us. We have prepared room for you."

Catherine replies, "That is very thoughtful. We just arrived, and Henri did not indicate any arrangements. We will come to your house."

Vincent says, "Let us get their luggage from Henri, and we will follow you." He goes to Henri and explains the plan, and Henri accompanies him to the parking lot to take the luggage out of his car and transfer it to the white rental car. Catherine, Joseph and Anthony join them, and they make the exchange. Catherine and Joseph get into the back seat, and Anthony sits in the front seat. Latonya drives up in a black Chrysler Imperial with her parents, her sister, and her children.

The two cars, Vincent following, pull out of the parking lot of the mortuary and start down the main road.

It is late afternoon, still light, so they can see where they are going. The road outside of town is lined with trees and goes along the shore of a large lake. You can see from one end to the other, and there are only two houses on the lake, actually mansions, one at either end. Latonya pulls up into the circular drive at the front of the house farthest from town. A pontoon plane is parked on the side yard, and a 45 foot yacht is moored in front of the house, at the end of a dock. The grounds are meticulously landscaped.

Latonya parks the black Chrysler by the front door, and her family gets out of the car. Vincent parks behind her. There is astonished silence in his car. He finally says, "Wow! So this is home!"

Latonya gestures to them to follow her up the stairs to the front door. As they enter the front door, they see an expansive foyer, a grand entrance into a living room with 15 foot ceilings, elaborate chandeliers, and mahogany beams. It is lavishly furnished, with sofas and chairs upholstered in satin brocade and velvet in a deep maroon that contrasts with the thick gray carpet. It is perfectly maintained, like the grounds, with the furniture arranged in sitting areas before a huge fireplace with a travertine mantle.

The faces of the family reveal their awe. A middle-aged man in a suit, probably around 45, rises up from one of the sofas and comes forward to meet them. He shakes hands with each of the visitors and introduces himself as a neighbor, James Murray.

Latonya introduces her parents and her sister, Malila, and the two families of strangers behave politely, yet awkwardly. Anthony always holds back, allowing Vincent to take the lead. It is apparent that Vincent is in charge. Catherine and Joseph are too shaken by the whole experience to do more than respond to direction. They are dumb-founded and shocked at this glimpse into their son's life.

The how and why the two families are there together is actually a mystery to all of them. The responsible party is stretched out in the coffin at the mortuary, in his prime, far too young to die, looking healthy. The hand of illness did not take him out. None of them welcomes the situation, none of them is prepared for it, and none of them wants to be a party to it. But there they are. And the two small boys, the youngest barely able to walk, cling to their mother, yet reach out to Vincent as if they know him. The truth is, he looks so much like Jacques that the boys feel as if he might be their father. And they comprehend nothing except their mother is very unhappy, that strangers are in their house, and that their father isn't there.

Latonya invites them to have a seat in the living room. She says, "This is Jacques' home, and you are his family. You are welcome to stay here. We have rooms for all of you."

Malila says, "Yes, as soon as we knew you were coming, we made a place for you. Jacques would want that."

Vincent says, "My grandparents can stay here. I refuse to stay in my father's house." He is visibly shaken with emotion. It is so overwhelming, the opulence, the contrast with his last experience of Jacques at the age of 5 in the shack in McGregor when he beat his mother. The hatred and resentment rise up in him, and there is no outlet. It wouldn't be fair to direct it to Latonya or her parents. This was his experience, more than twenty years earlier.

James Murray comes to Vincent and puts his hand on his shoulder and says: "Actually, I came here to invite you and your brothers to my home. I live at the other end of the lake. We have room for you. When will your other brother arrive?"

Vincent says, "Tomorrow. Frank is flying in from Germany. He is stationed there. It is very gracious for you to host us. We will accept. Thank you for the alternative. We have not had time to make hotel reservations. "

James says, "You can bring in your grandparents' luggage and then follow me."

Latonya and her family observe this exchange, and their faces express relief that at least some of the tension is resolved. Latonya was married to Jacques for only three years, had met him just a few month before. She knew nothing about the grown sons, nothing about his past life. He had mentioned that his parents lived in Ontario, but she had never met them. He spoke very little about his life before he knew her, and she didn't ask.

She was so caught up in the thrill of being singled out by such a wealthy and successful man, she revered him, never questioned him.

When he brought her to this house, said that it would be their home, that her parents and family were always welcome, she felt as if she were Cinderella and had found her prince.

Vincent and Anthony go out to the white Ford to get their grandparents' luggage. They carry it in, hug their grandparents, shake hands with Latonya's family. Vincent pats the oldest boy in the cheek and throws the youngest up in the air. They follow James out into the drive.

Chapter 38

Jacques was always able to compartmentalize, to contain his experience within strict parameters. In McGregor he could keep separate his work on the farm, his obligation to Shannon, his smuggling business, his "insurance" business, his relationship with Hungarian Joe, his relationship with Frenchie, his brief marriage to Francine. It enabled him not to commit to anyone but himself, to be able to walk away from any single compartment and not look back. He put his trust in no one completely, resented expectation of obligation, always anticipated violation or disappointment.

He knew he was clever and resourceful, charismatic, capable of molding and manipulating people according to his will. He discovered this when he was a small child, and he honed it throughout his life. It was his response to the rigidity offered by the upbringing by Catherine and Joseph. They knew only one way of life, the farm. They toiled from dawn to dusk, planted in perfect rows, harvested and sold in accordance with the season, raised livestock and butchered so successfully their slaughter house was known in Detroit and as far away as Toronto.

It was unthinkable to Joseph and Catherine that their son, their only child, could desire any other life. Even when they sent him to College, it was with the expectation it would make him a better farmer. It was unthinkable to Joseph and Catherine to do anything unethical or dishonest. They valued their reputation in the community, within the church, within their extended family. There was only one way to do business: the right way.

Jacques focused only on outcome. His actions, intentions, perceptions were not generated from ethical values. He was always deliberately on the fringe, evaluating success by achievement of each small step moving him forward to his desired outcome. He resented the restrictions that got in his way - the having to get married, the having to inherit his parents' life, the having to be boxed up in McGregor. When the resentment grew so strong he had to explode, he expressed it with brutality and violence, the brutality and violence he turned upon Shannon that Vincent witnessed.

Today, we might diagnose him as bi-polar, yet the kind of rage welling up within him has been the stuff of myth, of some of the most formidable of Celtic heroes, of Cuchulain, for instance. The "Mighty Cu" would go into a frenzy before he went into battle, and no enemy could overcome him. His unique weapon was the *gae bulga,* thrust from his foot. When it penetrated the opponent, it would explode inside of him.

Jacques' rage was Cu-like. He could control its onset. It was a tool he could use to intimidate when necessary. Once someone had experienced it, they would be wary of provoking it again. It gave him control. He was exceedingly charming, a great conversationalist with a quick sense of humor. People sought his company. When he entered the room, he took command. He was so "fast on his feet" no one could get the best of him. He made them laugh. With those who knew him well, who were most frequently in his company, like Hungarian Joe or Frenchie, he always had the edge because there was the fear of setting him off.

It was his charm and wit that empowered him to move into Montreal and to conquer the environment. He generated enthusiasm with his self confidence. It endeared him to the DuBois family who allowed him to enter by marriage. He had a way of looking at each deal as a challenge to be made to work. Even though he put his advantage first, he could articulate the opportunity so effectively that it was not apparent. People around him felt they were winning. He could read people.

And then there was the insurance. His first experience with the insurance company, burning down houses, cemented the concept into his practice. It became a natural part of every business or personal relationship he formed. He would take out an insurance policy on each person involved, with himself as the beneficiary. It was his security investment.

So when he invested in the race track, he made the insurance part of the finance deal. He had policies on both Frenchie and Hungarian Joe. When he came into the DuBois family, he took out insurance policies on Collette and the two brothers, on the mother. When he decided to move away from the gambling and the prostitution of the DuBois enterprise, into real estate development, insurance was at the core.

Jacques had travelled to Colorado in the United States at the invitation of a business associate who had a home in Aspen. He observed the success of the ski industry in that well-established mountain town. While he was there, he visited Vail, the man-made resort. With his love of hunting and fishing, he had explored the area surrounding Montreal, and frequently flew to Saint Jovite and Mount Tremblant in his plane for a one-day excursion.

It struck him that the area had a Vail-like potential that could be a "straight" business, or at least more "straight" than what he was doing with the DuBois brothers and the investors in the Carat Club. He invited a group of them together in a conference room in the Royal Hotel. He had a large map of the Saint Jovite and Mount Tremblant area. Frenchie and Hungarian Joe held it up against the wall.

He explained to them that he had just been in Colorado where they were building ski lifts and hotels. He had the idea they could do the same thing in Saint Jovite/Mount Tremblant, where there was only a small village with a few shops. The land was cheap.

One of the men commented: "No one in Canada is skiing."

Jacques replied: "It will take a few years for the ski craze to hit Canada. They are always ahead of us in the U.S. If we do this development right, we'll multiply the investment by at least ten times. The ski resort will immediately boost the value of the land."

Jacques answered each of their questions, cornered their concerns.

He had a ten year plan. They would establish a Holding Company and leverage half of the money coming in from the Club business for land acquisition. Each member would begin buying land individually with a pretense of building a second home, and each acquisition would be made in a separate company. That way they would not attract attention because they wanted the land to stay cheap. Each one would use a different real estate agent. The amount available for each acquisition would be based on the share the investors held in the Carat Club.

He succeeded in selling his idea. The two most crucial were his brothers-in-law who held the primary interest in the Club. When they assented, the bandwagon effect took over, and everyone wanted to be on board. Jacques made it clear that he would be the President of the Mount Tremblant Holding Company and the Chief Executive Officer. He would be scouting out the parcels of land and making the acquisition assignments. He would take the lead in negotiating with the bank for the loan to capitalize the endeavor. They were happy with that. No one else wanted to do it. They would all be passive recipients of Jacques' enterprise.

So that's how Jacques got to Saint Jovite. He took out a $500,000 life insurance policy on each of the investors, in the personal name of the investor, with the beneficiary Mount Tremblant Holding. The first parcel of land purchased was the spot on the north shore of the Lake where Jacques would build his home. It was acquired in a separate company in his name, and held within the Holding Company. Then Collette and her mother were killed in an automobile accident, and

Jacques was able to use the money from their life insurance policies to build the house.

That was about as "straight" as Jacques could be. People in Saint Jovite expected him to be coming and going as his house was built, and it gave him the opportunity to prospect for deals for land acquisition for members of his Holding Company. He was popular in the village, and soon everyone knew him. They considered him a widower, still very young and very eligible.

Latonya's family, Mohawk, had lived in Saint Jovite for generations. Her father and brothers were in the lumber business, and they provided the lumber for Jacques' house and the Holding Company resort projects. He got to know the family, and soon he was being "matched" with the raving beauty of the family, Latonya, with her raven black hair, her green eyes, and her voluptuous body. She was considerably younger than he was, but she was smart, unusually self-educated, bi-lingual, and knew the family business. They began spending more and more time together, and Jacques finally asked her to marry him.

He was the most happy he had ever been in his life. He enjoyed his work and he loved his young wife. She quickly became pregnant and gave him two sons. Hungarian Joe and Frenchie had made acquistions and moved to Saint Jovite. He was surrounded by family and friends, with insurance policies on all of them. The Holding Company was working and the building of the resort underway.

Chapter 39

Vincent follows James Murray's Mercedes along the shore of the lake up to the circular drive banked with Cyprus trees. They park before an opulent Tudor mansion with majestic turrets dominating the far side of the lake. The entrance to the house faces a carefully manicured lawn that stretches to the lake where a 60 foot yacht is docked, as well as a canoe and a kayak. Vincent parks the white Ford behind the white Mercedes. A servant comes out of the house to meet them. He salutes James, shakes hands with Vincent and Anthony, and then picks up the luggage to carry it inside.

The two brothers enter the front hallway and gaze over the rich red carpet of the living room, decorated with 18th century furnishings, paintings, and antiques. The living room adjoins a library with floor to ceiling books bound in leather, accessible by ladder.

Vincent remarks: "I've never seen so many books in one house."

James replies: "Some are mine and some are part of my late father's collection. We were both educated at Cambridge in England, and we find comfort in being surrounded by them. They are our friends."

An attractive middle-aged woman, wearing a calf-length white dress , enters the library from the hallway and holds out her hands in greeting. James says, "This is my wife, Marjorie."

Marjorie says, "Welcome to our home. Please accept our condolences for the death of your father."

Vincent and Anthony come forward and shake hands with her. Vincent says, "Thank you. We so appreciate your hospitality."

Marjorie gestures toward James: "I will let James show you where you will be sleeping. You must be tired and hungry."

James points to the hallway and says, "Please follow me. We want you to be comfortable." James leads Vincent and Anthony down a set of wide stairs, also carpeted in red, to a large billiard room with a bar and a fireplace. He directs Vincent to the first open door on the left and Anthony to the first open door on the right. He says, "Here are your rooms."

Vincent and Anthony each stand in the doorway of their room and peer in to see both furnished with a double bed, a desk, a dresser, an upholstered chair, and a luggage rack. Each one's luggage already rests on the rack. Each bedroom has a separate bath.

Anthony says, "Oh, this is wonderful. Thank you for your generous hospitality."

Vincent adds, "Yes, we are so grateful to you."

James says, "Please make yourselves at home. The bar is yours. Take anything you like. I know you have been travelling for the last two days and will want to unwind. We'll have a light supper here this evening so that you can relax.I will light a fire. It gets chilly here at night."

The servant is already setting the table. Vincent and Anthony go into their rooms to get themselves settled. When they emerge, James is standing behind the bar. He asks, "What will you have?"

The "light" supper turns out to be grilled pork chops, apple sauce, fresh green beans, and apple pie. After dinner they sit by the fire, each in a large leather chair, enjoying an after-dinner drink. Anthony gets up and yawns: "I think I need to call it a day. " He goes to his bedroom and closes the door. Vincent and James remain seated.

James says, "How about another scotch?"

Vincent replies: "Thank you. I have so many thoughts running through my head, I won't be able to sleep yet."

James gets up, goes to the bar, picks up the bottle of scotch, and fills their glasses. He sets the bottle down on the table in front of them. He asks, "Have you ever been to Saint Jovite before, Vincent?"

Vincent strangely feels he can confide in James and says, "No. I haven't been with my father since I was five years old. He became very violent, beat my mother and broke her feet. My grandmother came to rescue us, and we escaped to Detroit. I watched it all, and I vowed I would kill him. My brothers were so young, they didn't even know him. We never saw him again."

James asks, "Then why have you even come to this funeral?

Vincent replies, "We came to the funeral because my grandparents asked us to come. They didn't want to be alone. This whole situation frightens them. He was their only son. When they called me, then I asked my brothers. Anthony lives near me in California, and Frank is stationed in Germany, in Stuttgart. He will be here tomorrow."

James asks, "Do you know any of the people here?"

Vincent replies, "We don't know any of the people at the mortuary. We are all very confused. We don't know anything about our father's business. We didn't know about this wife or the little boys. My father never told my grandparents about his life here or invited them here. They are just plain farmers from McGregor. We had no idea he was so wealthy or lived so lavishly. They knew he had a plane, but that's all."

James asks, "Are you aware how much you resemble him?"

Vincent says, "My grandparents never mentioned it. I had no idea. They knew not to talk to me about him. I visited them often at the farm, but they didn't have pictures of him out when I was there. I was taken aback at the mortuary by the way people reacted to me. Then I saw him in the coffin."

James says, "It must be like looking in a mirror."

Vincent replies, "One of those men in the black suits came and kissed me on both cheeks. Did he think I was Jacques? It creeps me out."

James comments, "Jacques was a very forceful man. He always attracted attention no matter what he did. We have done business over the years, and I came to know him well. I was his banker. That's how we happened to buy the lake and build our houses on it. Until the last few years, when things became a bit murky, I had a glimpse into most of his affairs, some good, some not so good."

Vincent is curious: "When you say "murky," do you mean the guys in the black suits. They do a lot of whispering among themselves, and they appear not to have anything to do with his wife's family."

James refills their glasses and replies, "I don't know them. I saw them for the first time early this afternoon when I stopped by the mortuary to pay my respects. My family and I have kept in touch with Jacques and his family. We share the same lake. When Latonya told me your grandparents were coming with three of their grandsons, I offered to have you stay here. She has her family at the house, too."

Vincent says, "We were planning to stay at a hotel, but we knew nothing about Saint Jovite. This is so much better. Thank you."

Returning to the subject of the men in the black suits, James remarks, "You can be sure Jacques was involved with something, probably several things. He was an adventurer. He couldn't stand still."

Vincent observes, "His wife is a real looker, but very young. She can't be any older than I am."

James says, " I know for sure she's number five. That's a part of not being able to sit still. He told me he was married twice in McGregor and then twice in Montreal. His second Montreal wife was killed in a car accident. This one is a Mohawk, a native of Saint Jovite."

Vincent notes, "Her relatives don't seem to like us, especially me."

James observes, "It may be because two of her brothers died a few months ago in one of your father's planes. They were with two of your father's old friends whom I did know: Frenchie and Hungarian Joe. I don't know the details, but there was a rumor around town that Jacques had an insurance policy on every one of them, with himself as the beneficiary. You look so much like Jacques, they are probably projecting their attitude toward him on to you."

Vincent reflects: "That would explain why they are all so hostile, even though I am not Jacques. They don't like the men in the black suits, either. And actually, neither do I. They seem to have an agenda that has nothing to do with mourning. Jacques must have still been doing the same business. My mother gave me my baby book when I turned 25. On my first birthday, she wrote: 'Today is your first birthday, and Daddy burned down our house.' She said that's how he made money when I was a baby, burning down houses for the insurance companies."

James replies, "As I said, it was a rumor. I can't verify it, and I certainly wouldn't ask, especially now. Those Mohawks look right through you with their black eyes. "

Chapter 40

It was overload for Vincent, all of this information about the father he never knew. For the first time he questioned his decision to reject Jacques' offer to come to Montreal. He never considered it. Whenever Jacques' name was mentioned, the childhood hatred would rise up in him. It was apparent Jacques had been very successful monetarily. Vincent had many questions about the men in the black suits at the mortuary. Who were they? What was their relationship with Jacques? Why was he kissed on both cheeks?

Shannon had indoctrinated him with the idea that his father would always be "up to no good." She had also always harped on the discrimination of his grandparents, that they liked him more than Anthony or Frank, that they only encouraged him to visit them. When his Uncle told him of Jacques' offer, Shannon was angry that Jacques only wanted Vincent, not the other two boys. For the first time the issue of "what was fair" popped into Vincent's mind.

He had no idea how much he resembled physically the man in the coffin. It made him wonder if he resembled him in other ways as well. He knew he was nothing like Shannon. He loved his mother and respected her for providing a home for him, but their personalities were totally different. Shannon and his stepfather fought every Sunday. She was never satisfied.

From the time Vincent had his first paper route, he was

independent. He paid his own tuition at the Catholic schools, all the way through to St. Patrick's. He never took a report card home for his mother to sign. It was none of her business. He delivered the *Detroit Times* and Anthony delivered the *Free Press*. Anthony was always late with his papers, and Vincent would go to his customers and get them to change papers. Shannon resented that, said he was "picking on" Anthony.

If he depended on anyone in the Irish side of his family, it was Mick and Kelly, especially Mick. He had such a kind heart, and he always encouraged Vincent, helped him buy his first car. He set a good example for reliability, always on time for work, never missed a day. He had the wit of the Irish, always seeing the quixotic side of things, never holding a grudge. His mother held grudges.

But when his grandparents called and asked him to come to Montreal with them for the funeral, Shannon encouraged him to go and insisted that he bring his brothers. She thought there might be something there. She didn't know. She really didn't know. Vincent's first impression was that Jacques' affairs were convoluted and even his young wife didn't have a clue what he was doing. He was sure James Murray would tell him more.

Vincent's life since that 50th anniversary party had taken many turns. He got in a terrible fight at St. Patrick's and badly injured one of the boys. Father Donnoley made him paint his office and threw him out of school. He applied to the Jesuits, thinking he would try the priesthood, but they wouldn't take him. His parents were divorced. But he did get accepted by the Brothers of Notre Dame, and they sent him to Watertown, Wisconsin, to a boys' school, a boarding school for the children of the wealthy brewers.

Vincent couldn't completely take the vow of poverty, and he hid money in his shoe when he arrived. His first job was cleaning the barn, and he did such a good job, the brother in charge of the farm asked for him to be assigned to him. He took the job on the condition he could hunt in the afternoon with the shotgun in the barn. So every day when his chores were done, he went out into the field and shot pheasants. Some of the brothers complained about the noise, but none of them complained about the pheasant on the table for dinner.

He had to be a high school graduate to be a novitiate, so he finished his diploma the first three months, learning Latin overnight – not telling them he had studied Latin all through high school. They thought he was brilliant. He made friends with some of the brothers, especially Brothers Lambert and Fitzpatrick. Brother Lambert weighed 500 pounds and couldn't bend down to reach his shoes. Vincent would tie his shoes every morning. When Mick and Shannon came to visit the school, Brother Fitzpatrick and Mick stood for many minutes repeating each other's names, Mick Clancy and James H. Fitzpatrick.

Vincent didn't last there. He and a friend got busted for buying beer with the money in his shoe and hiding it in a cornfield. Brother Lambert came walking across the cornfield and asked for the cigarettes. His stupid friend, Ronnie, said, "We don't have cigarettes. We have beer." That got Vincent a whole night on his knees. In fact, he had callouses on his knees from asking forgiveness. The final straw was the string of letters he received. The Brother in charge said they were from girls, that Vincent was too "worldly" to keep the vow of chastity. He was right.

He went from Watertown back to Detroit and lived at home with Shannon and his stepfather. He took a job at the U.S. Gypsum Company in River Rouge, starting as the pay roll clerk. It gave him a chance to know everyone in the plant, and he started a bowling league, even inviting the President of the company to bowl with them. One of his jobs before Stein and Stein was setting pins at a bowling alley, and he was a good bowler. He wrote the "Bowling News," and everyone looked forward to its publication to see if their name would be listed.

One day he happened to be talking to the Head of Engineering who had a problem with cooking the stucco. Vincent put on a hard hat and went with him. They were cooking the high vat of stucco from the bottom only. Vincent suggested that if they had the burner in the middle and at the top, the stucco would cook more quickly and evenly. The Head engineer was so impressed he made Vincent an engineer.

All the while Vincent was working at the U.S Gypsum company, he was going to school at night and working part-time at Sears. The company paid half his tuition if he got a C. He was bringing back A's, and the President of the company was impressed by him. Vincent probably would have had a sound future with the company, but Uncle

Sam came to call. It was the cusp between the Korean and the Viet Nam War, and the draft was in force. Vincent needed four classes to be exempt for education, and he had cut back to three classes. He got drafted. His grandparents said, "Come home to Canada. You are a Canadian citizen." He was. With a Canadian father and an American mother, he had dual citizenship.

He elected to serve and entered the U.S. Army out of Detroit. He was in his early twenties, older than most draftees. The first thing they did was pass a basket so that they could release their "armor." The basket went around four times before all of the knives and guns were deposited. It was a tough crew. On the way to Fort Leonard Wood for basic training, several of the men jumped the train. Not Vincent.

All of those years practicing his shooting in order to kill Jacques stood Vincent in good stead in the army. He was an expert shot, and the sergeant used him to train the other men. In one of the training missions, the sergeant put him in the front of 600 men for a forced march at 30 degrees below zero. He asked for live ammunition to use if anyone fell out. No one did. The men suffered frost bite, and the sergeant was court-martialed for mistreating them. Vincent proved the effectiveness of his leadership.

Toward the end of his basic training, Vincent saw a sign for "Chaplains," and he thought, "That's the closest to God and the farthest from the front." He applied. When the men were assigned after basic training, his whole unit went to Korea, except Vincent, who went to Fort Ord for Chaplain training. He had requested a resume and letter of recommendation when he left U.S. Gypsum. When he completed Chaplain training, he used them to secure a position as Head Chaplain Assistant for the Colonel at Fort Lewis.

He was a Catholic working for the Protestants, in charge of the money for the Colonel. He had a colorful experience there, making friends and enemies. He "accidently" threw a sergeant they all called the "chief jerk" into a safe and broke his ribs. The sergeant retaliated by getting Vincent orders to ship to Viet Nam. The Colonel had the orders changed. He was getting ready to retire, and he didn't have a clue what Vincent was doing, only that they had more money then ever before.

Vincent was saved. The orders sent him for parachute training, and the life expectancy in Viet Nam was 15 minutes. All of the time Vincent was at Fort Lewis, he had been taking college classes. His Colonel wanted to recommend him to West Point, but Vincent wanted out. He had married, got two months early discharge for his college classes, and wanted to move to California. He got a job at Douglas Aircraft in Long Beach, and he had his first child.

On one of his leaves, he had visited the U.S. Gypsum Company. He asked for some of his buddies, men with whom Vincent had paid for a fishing trip into the bush in Canada, on an isolated and un-fished lake. They were being flown in. When Vincent got drafted, they refunded his money. The men all drowned and never came back from that trip. Uncle Sam had saved him!

Chapter 41

Vincent is with James Murray for three nights, and each night they sit and drink scotch and talk. It doesn't interest Anthony and Frank, who had arrived from Germany, wearing his Army uniform. They play pool, or watch television, or just go to bed. For the first time, Vincent is learning about his father, the man in the coffin. James Murray's family had founded the Royal Bank of Scotland, and he had been president for many years. Vincent is impressed that he knew his father so well and respected him.

James tells him that Jacques' great passion was hunting and fishing and that he was an accomplished bush pilot. He would go out in the wilderness with Frenchie and Hungarian Joe to shoot elk or moose or deer. They flew all over Canada and into the Upper Peninsula of Michigan and Minnesota. He always brought the Murray family game from his trips. He asks if Vincent shares his father's love of the wilderness and shooting.

Vincent tells him: "I've always been a good hunter. My grandfather gave me a gun when I was nine. Whenever I went to visit my grandparents in Canada, I would go hunting. They have lots of game on the farm – pheasants, ducks, geese, deer. My grandmother loved to cook whatever I took down. Since I've been in California, I've gone on two long-range fishing trips to Mexico, ten days, fishing for tuna, sea bass and wahoo. They call me the cannibal of the boat!"

James continues: "Jacques was a complicated man. He had such a great love for the outdoors, always arranging expeditions to untouched places. He could have been a guide. But he was all business, and when you did business with him, he made the rules and you followed them. It got to be too much for me, and I pulled out. That's why we could still be friends. He was very fond of my wife, Marjorie."

Vincent responds: "That makes him seem almost human. He was so cruel to my mother that I always intended to kill him. I used to practice. He did take me pheasant hunting twice when I was five, before we escaped from Canada to Detroit. I actually liked him then. But after he broke my mother's feet, I hated him. I wouldn't let my grandparents say his name around me."

James says, "I have experienced his rage when he didn't get his way. He didn't talk about his past life and seldom shared anything personal. He kept his business totally separate from his life here in Saint Jovite. I don't know what he was like before he came here. I had no idea that he had grown sons like you. After I stopped handling his banking, I knew nothing except what happened here locally. It must feel strange for you to be here now. Do you have any good memories?"

Vincent reflects: "I only knew him for a very short time, a time when my parents were not happy with each other, when they were both frustrated and stuck with each other. Now that I am older, I can understand some of it. My mother got pregnant with me when she was 15, and they had to get married. Then she had two more boys by the time I was five. He was a butcher and a farmer and probably didn't like either one. My grandparents wanted me to move to Canada and take over the farm when I was drafted. I couldn't see myself trapped on the farm."

James says, "I can't even imagine Jacques as a farmer. If I hadn't had business dealings with him, I would have regarded him the same way the town did: a wealthy real estate developer with a beautiful young wife, two small boys, a great hunter, and a great host."

"Well," replies Vincent, "That's a world away from life in McGregor. It's a very small town, mostly all farmers, mostly all Catholic, mostly all related. Everybody knows everybody's business. There were seven girls in my grandmother's family, and they married seven brothers. They are all farmers. My grandmother's father gave each of them a farm. They never really leave town except maybe to go across the Ambassador Bridge to Detroit. When they entertain, they entertain each other. I always feel related to everyone when I go there, although I haven't been back for several years. California is a totally different lifestyle."

"Jacques loved to entertain, " comments James. "You probably noticed that long driveway into his house. He had that wired with electricity so that he could thaw out the snow at any time of the year. I remember last Christmas when he led a whole marching band up that driveway and into the house for the Christmas party. He invited half the town. He had the driveway lined with red and green Christmas lights, and all of the musicians were wearing red hats and green scarves, as was Jacques. The guests were already in the house, and they came out on the porch to greet him and the musicians.

They were playing Jingle Bells as they entered, and everyone joined in singing. He had the foyer all decorated with holly and Christmas lights, and he had a 15 foot Christmas tree in the Great Room with the high beams. Latonya stood at the door in a long, red dress.

They served the guests hot cider and mulled wine, and they had a buffet table with ham and turkey with all the trimmings and another table with Christmas cookies and desserts. The band played Christmas carols, and everyone sang. It was a beautiful party. Now that you've met her, you can imagine how gorgeous Latonya looked, and she was so completely happy and proud."

Vincent asks, "When did they get married?"

"They've actually only been married for about three years," James replies. "Jacques acknowledged to me that she was number five, but I don't know whether he ever told Latonya. He said he wanted to get it right this time. He was thrilled when she got pregnant almost immediately, and he adored the two boys. He never spoke about the past marriages or children from other marriages, and I didn't ask."

Vincent says, " I knew about a second wife in McGregor. My grandparents had a picture of a daughter. When he had my uncle invite me to Montreal, he was married. I assume that's the wife that was killed in the automobile accident. He must have sandwiched another one in there somewhere. He obviously had a way with women."

"Yes, he was a charmer, " James replies. "He totally swept Marjorie off her feet. She would get excited every time he stopped by to bring us game and fish after his trips. But he was totally committed to a new life here. The only past elements were his partners in the ski resort, the men in the black suits, and his buddies, Frenchie and Hungarian Joe who moved here. Frenchie and Hungarian Joe were always with him on the hunting and fishing trips. He was definitely in total mourning when the plane went down with them and Latonya's brothers in it. I truly believe it was a freak accident, that Jacques had nothing to do with it, even though there were the insurance policies. "

"We'll never know now," Vincent observes.

Chapter 42

The established "groups" are standing in the parking lot of the mortuary, waiting for it to open: the men in the black suits, Latonya and her family, and Vincent and family, now joined by a cousin, Renee, from McGregor, especially to support Catherine. A flatbed truck drives down the street and pulls into the parking lot. It carries a flower wreath 30 feet tall and 30 feet wide, shaped as a wheel, divided into five spokes with one spoke cut out. The flowers are roses, carnations, and chrysanthemums. What is that story by D.H. Lawrence, the "Odor of Chrysanthemums," the flowers of death.

It takes the driver and five other men to unload the wreath and place it by the door of the mortuary. It would be impossible to get it through the door. The men in the black suits express their satisfaction, and the two families stare with astonishment. Anthony says, "That could be in the Rose Bowl Parade." Vincent surmises, based on his conversation with James Murray and his experience with Henri, that Jacques is the missing spoke, and the men in the black suits are the rest of the wheel.

Catherine asks, "Who do you suppose are the other four?" Vincent replies, "They have to be Henri and his friends in the black suits."

Renee remarks, "I recognized the men in black suits here in the parking lot. They were all in the dining room at the hotel last night when I had my dinner, two tables of them, one with just four and another long table with the rest. I couldn't help but notice. We were the only ones in the dining room, and they were very loud, arguing about money and who would pay for the funeral. Now I get it that it was this funeral. The one that talks to you, Henri, passed a basket down the long table, and they all put in money."

Joseph says, "They must have used it to pay for the wreath, too. I've wondered about the money for the funeral. No one has spoken to me. It has seemed awkward to ask Latonya, she has so much else to attend to, with a house full of people. Henri appears to be in charge, and if he wants money from us, he will probably ask. I'm not going to volunteer. We're outsiders here."

Vincent hasn't exactly had a "change of heart" about Jacques, but his conversations with James have created a sense of Jacques' personality and somehow a feeling of connection enough to at least make him curious about the cause of death. Henri said he had a heart attack. Jacques was only in his later forties, and he had certainly been healthy enough to go on all of those hunting and fishing trips. He knows sometimes even younger and apparently healthy people have heart attacks, but the spoke cut out of the wheel makes him suspicious. Whose idea was it to get rid of the spoke?

He says to the family, "You go on inside. I'm going to stop by the office of the doctor who attended to Jacques at the hospital. I called ahead and made an appointment."

Vincent gets in the white Ford and drives off down the road. James has given him directions to the doctor's office, located near the hospital.

He is in the waiting room only long enough for the doctor to finish with the patient before him. The nurse invites him into the office, and he sits down in the chair across from the desk. The doctor comes in, shakes hands with Vincent, and sits behind the desk.

Vincent says, "I won't take much of your time. I am here to learn the results of the autopsy."

The doctor replies, "In Canada we are not required to do an autopsy. The cause of death was natural."

Vincent says, "How can you prove that?"

The doctor answers, "The man's heart stopped beating. It was cardiac arrest."

Vincent asks, "But what caused the arrest? There appear to be some interested players."

The doctor's face is red and his hands are shaking. Vincent can hear him breathing. He won't look Vincent in the eye when he replies, "I am a medical man. I have only my medical opinion based on my medical expertise. That is all I know."

Vincent leaves, now convinced that the men in the black suits are the cause of death. He's heard that it is possible to pump air into someone's veins to cause a heart attack. He really doesn't have a clue. Saint Jovite is not the sort of place to get an "expert" opinion.

What Renee didn't overhear in the dining room was the

conversation Henri was having with the three men at his table. He told them: "After the funeral, we will meet back in Montreal at 2:00 p.m. the next day in the office. I have the papers for the Holding Company. In the meantime, I'm passing the basket to pay for the mortuary and the funeral."

There is dissension, distrust, an unraveling for lack of a leader. Jacques had been in charge since the founding of the Holding Company. He scouted out the properties for acquisition. He oversaw the incorporation of the individual companies. He oversaw the development of the ski resort. He went back and forth between Montreal and Saint Jovite, but he was hands-on at the site. He ran everything, and the "investors" were essentially passive investors

His brothers-in-law did not interfere. They ran that Carat Club and entrusted the investment in the Holding Company totally to Jacques. They continued to have a close relationship with Jacques after the fatal accident with their sister and mother, but since Jacques and Collette had no children, he wasn't tied to the extended family as closely as he would have been. The DuBois brothers only had visited Saint Jovite twice, and although they knew about the marriage to Latonya, they had never met her. Hungarian Joe and Frenchie were the most involved with the construction at the site, but now they were gone. The brothers chose not to attend the funeral. They didn't know the cause of death, who was up to what, and didn't want to know.

Henri had been Jacques' "gofer," his messenger boy, and now he was taking charge, or attempting to take charge. His position was shaky at best. There were too many questions. He and the three men at the table couldn't agree within themselves. They asked: "What kind of insurance policy did Jacques have?" "Whose name is on the house?"

One remarked: "If you have all the papers, you can pay for the funeral."

Henri replied, "I'm taking a collection for the wreath and the funeral . We'll discuss the way forward at the meeting, just the four of us, and we'll tell the rest."

Chapter 43

The last viewing of the body is the morning before the funeral. The people begin to leave and get into their cars. A driver brings the hearse to the front door, and the Director of the mortuary asks people to stand aside so that the coffin can be loaded into the hearse. Six of the men in black suits carry the coffin to the hearse and load the coffin. The hearse pulls out, followed by the flatbed truck carrying the wreath with the spoke cut out. The cars fall into line, the family cars first.

Latonya is wearing black, as do all of her immediate family. Drivers open the doors of the black Chrysler Imperial and a Rolls Royce for them. Vincent drives the white Ford with Catherine, Joseph, and Renee in the back seat and Anthony and Frank in the front seat. Frank wears his Army uniform. The procession proceeds down the main street of Saint Jovite to the Catholic Church. The hearse stops by the front door of the church. The same six men go to the hearse, open the back door, lift out the coffin, and carry it into the church. They place it in front of the altar. The truck with the wreath drives on to the burial site.

People park their cars and get out, standing aside to let the family go into the church before them. Latonya and her family sit in the front row on the right side of the church. Joseph, Catherine, Renee, Anthony and Frank sit in the front row of the left side. There is an open space in the pew, reserved for Vincent. The "mourners" stream into the church and take seats in the pews. An organist plays hymns as they enter. The room settles in, quiets down, in expectation for the funeral service to begin. The organist plays "The Old Rugged Cross," said to be Jacques' favorite.

Vincent has gone to the small room behind the altar to speak with the priest. The priest is in his robe, ready to go out to start the service. Vincent confronts him: "How can you give this man a Catholic service and burial. He has been married five times. It is against the teaching of the Church."

The priest replies, "I did not know the man. He was not a member of this parish. I have been asked to perform a funeral, and I am doing my duty as a priest."

The organist continues to play "The Old Rugged Cross." It is the signal for the priest to enter the sanctuary. The people in the pews look impatiently and anxiously at the altar and whisper among themselves about when the service will begin.

Vincent will not let the priest go. He persists: "I insist that this service be stopped. The man does not deserve a Catholic funeral."

The organist continues to play "The Old Rugged Cross." Joseph gets up out of his seat in the front pew, walks to the altar, and goes behind it. He enters the room where Vincent berates the priest.

Joseph says, "When are you starting the service?"

The priest replies: " I am ready. This young man has stopped me, insisting that the man does not deserve a Catholic service."

Joseph says, "I am his father, and I want the service to go on. It would break his mother's heart not to have it here in the church. Vincent, please go out and take your seat."

Vincent, his face red with rage, gives in: "I will obey your wishes, but it is wrong."

The organist again plays "The Old Rugged Cross." The congregation continues to look anxiously at the altar. Vincent and Joseph come out from behind the altar and take their seat. The priest comes out and begins the service: "We have come here today to celebrate the life of Jacques Pascal. Please stand and let us pray." He crosses himself.

The congregation rises, cross themselves. Latonya weeps. She holds the baby in her lap and has her arm around her other son. The service ends. The same six men carry the coffin out to the hearse parked by the front door of the church. They load the coffin into the hearse. Latonya's family leaves the church and get into their cars. Joseph and Catherine, followed by the sons and Renee, leave the church and get into the white Ford. The family cars follow the hearse down the road to the graveside. James and Marjorie Murray follow the families in the white Mercedes. The procession stretches down the main street of Saint Jovite out into the countryside to the cemetery where the burial will take place.

The 30 foot wreath with the fifth spoke cut out stands at the head of the open grave as the families exit their cars and approach the graveside. It has started to rain, a steady drizzle. People open the trunks of their cars to take out umbrellas.

The families sit in chairs beside the grave. The others stand behind them. The grave-digger stands to the side as the same pall bearers carry the coffin to the graveside. The grave-digger is wearing bib overalls and rubber boots up to the top of his thighs.

The priest arrives, and the families stand. The priest says, "Let us pray." He crosses himself. The service proceeds, and the rain continues to fall. When it is over, only Vincent stays behind to watch the grave-digger lower the coffin. As the grave-digger turns the crank, the train passes by and its whistle shrieks into the early evening darkness. The scene is eerie, almost grotesque, the kind of story one creates for Halloween night.

Vincent shudders. He says out loud, "I have always hated trains."

The sound of the whistle took him back to the farm, to the time he was alone in the field at his grandparents. When the train went by, he had a feeling of total anguish that he couldn't explain. It was something that rose up in him, that filled him with a great sadness. It might have been a premonition of this moment.

One Christmas, his mother gave him a train set. He said to her, "Why did you give this to me? I hate trains." He had no direct experience with trains, so the emotions he felt came from some place deep in his subconscious, as though that whistle was a preparation for this moment. His emotional state was raw. The man he had wanted to kill had just been lowered into the grave.

Yet the man he wanted to kill was not the man lowered in the grave. The man he wanted to kill was the man he knew at five years old. In his evenings with James Murray, Vincent had come to know another man, the man Jacques had become, larger than life, involved in business activities apparently shady, yet with monetary success and vision and leadership people respected. Vincent shared his love of the wilderness. He observed genuine love for the young wife and two sons, a man in recovery. Vincent felt sudden forgiveness and sorrow.

Chapter 44

Latonya invites everyone at the funeral to come to their home. They park down the long driveway and pour into the house, leaving their umbrellas on the porch. It is a party Jacques would have liked, would have given, would have wanted to be given. Platters of food are on the tables, some of it prepared from the game in the freezer from Jacques' hunting and fishing trips – venison, moose, elk, walleye, trout, pheasant, goose. Latonya has deliberately set about making this a feast in honor of Jacques.

They have an open bar with a bar tender. They do not hold back. Every request is honored, and the beer, wine, scotch, bourbon, gin and vodka flow, along with Canadian whisky. The people of Saint Jovite mingle with the people of Montreal. As is usually true at funerals, the memories they talk about are the good ones.

Latonya greets the guests as an elegant hostess. Vincent observes the men in the black suits come, stick together, do not mingle with the others, but take especial interest in the house. They have never been in it before. Vincent has a sudden premonition, not unlike the shriek of the train whistle, that the house will not belong to Latonya, that these men have either already taken possession or will soon take possession. He sees nothing generating from them except darkness.

The guests eat well, drink well, and begin to depart out into the rain and the night. The two families remain, re-gathering themselves after the stress of the day. Outside the rain is violent with loud claps of thunder and lightening.

A loud knock is heard on the front door: boom, boom, boom.

It is repeated: boom, boom, boom.

It is repeated again: boom, boom, boom.

Catherine is closest to the door. She wears a long black dress and her usual black oxfords. She walks to the door and opens it. The gravedigger stands there, his hip boots up to his thighs covered in mud, a shovel in his right hand. The lightening flashes across the lake to highlight his presence, a bolt of thunder echoes into the house. The gravedigger says: The corpse is buried. I've come to be paid."

Catherine says, "Come back tomorrow. Not tonight." She slams the door.

Vincent observes the scene, thinks, "I always wanted to kill him. They did it for me."

This isn't the only thing Vincent is thinking. He has been observing the dynamics of the parties in Saint Jovite for three days, filling in the gaps with the things James Murray has revealed to him. It has created a portrait of the father he really didn't know. He remembers both Hungarian Joe and Frenchie from his childhood in McGregor. Hungarian Joe always wore the same flat hat. Frenchie always brought him a treat, something sweet. They and his father were inseparable then.

Since they moved to Saint Jovite, hunted and fished with Jacques, remained such close friends and partners through all those years, it is unthinkable that Jacques would have wanted them killed in that plane crash just to collect the insurance. Latonya's brothers went down in the same crash. He would not have wished to be a cause of grief for his new wife. It didn't add up.

The death of Jacques is a mystery. There was no history of heart disease, no symptoms of illness observed by anyone. How did it happen? Why did it happen? Four spokes in a wheel wanted the fifth spoke out of the way. Would they have also wanted Hungarian Joe and Frenchie out of the way? Were the brothers just an "accidental" addition?

There is little to no communication between Latonya and the men in the black suits. Henri informed her about logistics for the funeral. He had at one point asked Latonya about the ownership of the house, whether it was in her name. She looked at him with a blank stare. Jacques took care of everything. She had no idea about his business or his ownership.

Vincent has bonded with the two boys. His resemblance to their father makes him familiar, raises expectations of attention and affection, and Vincent offers both. He loves children. It was a bit more difficult with Latonya. She came on to him. He doesn't know whether it is conscious or unconscious, but it makes him uncomfortable. He has his own family in California. He doesn't know how he could protect this family. It isn't his job, but he is the oldest son.

After the gravedigger's visit, the three brothers leave for their last night at the Murrays, going out in the rain. James and Marjorie Murray have already retired, and they are preparing to leave in the morning. In the morning, they thank their Murray hosts, express their gratitude for their hospitality. James Murray says, "Our pleasure. We are pleased to have known you, and we wish you well."

They go to the house to help Joseph and Catherine with their luggage and to say goodbye to Latonya and her family. Henri is driving Joseph, Catherine, Frank and Renee to the airport. Vincent and Anthony are returning their rental car to Montreal.

As they enter the foyer, the oldest boy runs to Vincent and begs to be picked up. Vincent picks him up and tosses him into the air. Latonya joins them. Vincent puts down the boy and pulls her aside to a quiet corner of the living room. Vincent says, "You need to be thinking about leaving here. I suggest you take the boys and go to your parents' home."

Latonya replies, "I don't want to leave here. This is our home."

Vincent is persistent: "I have been observing your husband's associates over the last few days. They are not going to allow you to keep this house. Renee overheard some of their conversations at the hotel. I believe you are in danger, you and your sons. "

Latonya responds, "I can take care of myself. Why don't you stay here with us?"

Vincent had been dreading this invitation. Latonya is asking him to move in and to take over Jacques' role in the family. There is no taking over Jacques' role in the business. That is wiped out. Latonya is an extraordinarily beautiful young woman, made only more attractive by her vulnerability.

Vincent reminds her: "I have my own family waiting for me in California. This is the last time I will ever see you. I do not want you to be in danger."

The oldest boy comes back and grabs Vincent's leg. He picks him up again and throws him in the air. He picks up the youngest one and throws him up, too. He is filled with affection and compassion for this family, and the sense of dread.

Chapter 45

Henri pulls up behind the white Ford and comes up the steps to the front door. He rings the bell, and the servant answers. As he enters the foyer, he greets Catherine, Joseph, and Renee. He shakes hand with the Vincent, Anthony, and Frank. He nods to Latonya's parents, and lightly embraces Latonya. He turns to Catherine and Joseph and asks: "Are you ready to leave?'

Joseph says, "Yes, our bags are ready. Frank is coming with us to catch his plane back to Germany."

Vincent says, "Anthony and I have a few stops to make in town before we leave. You go on ahead with our grandparents and Frank. Their plane reservations are later this afternoon. We don't leave Montreal until tomorrow morning. We're just staying at the Holiday Inn by the airport tonight."

Henri nods to Anthony and Vincent and replies: "I am sorry we had to meet under these circumstances, but it is my pleasure to know you. Please travel safely back to California. I will see to it that Catherine, Joseph and Renee are on the plane this afternoon and that Frank catches his flight."

Catherine and Joseph embrace Latonya, hug the boys, shake hands with Latonya's family and move toward the door. The servant opens the door, assists Catherine down the stairs. Henri opens his trunk, and

Vincent and Anthony load suitcases. Frank takes his suitcase out of the trunk of the white Ford and loads it into Henri's car. They all get in, Henri and Joseph in the front seat, Catherine, Frank, and Renee in the back seat. Henri gets behind the wheel, and the black car pulls out of the drive and starts down the road alongside the lake.

Vincent and Anthony say their good-byes. The baby reaches out for Vincent, and the older boy grabs on to his legs. Vincent throws each of them up in the air for the last time. They squeal with delight. Vincent goes to Latonya and embraces her. He says, "Please pay attention to what I have said."

The servant opens the front door, and the two young men turn and walk out the door. Vincent gets into the driver's seat, Anthony into the passenger seat. They both wave to Latonya's family gathered on the porch. Vincent pulls the white Ford out of the drive, down the road alongside the lake, passing through Saint Jovite on the way to the highway to Montreal. They aren't making any stops. Vincent just said that they were because he didn't want to follow Henri.

This whole trip has been disconcerting and unsettling. They came to a funeral of the father they really didn't know. They found themselves in a situation they didn't understand but which felt somehow sinister. Vincent has been kissed on both cheeks, and he doesn't believe that the men in the black suits are through with him. He is the oldest son. He is leaving behind his father's young family whose future he considers threatened.

As he drives along, he constantly checks the rear view mirror. A few miles outside of Saint Jovite, on the highway to Montreal, he observes a car following closely behind them with four men in the car. He says to Anthony: "I'm pretty sure we are being followed. Don't turn around and look. I'm going to speed up to see if I can shake them."

Vincent speeds up more, and the car behind speeds up more as well. The car behind bumps the back fender of the white Ford. The driver motions to Vincent to pull over at the side of the road. Vincent accelerates. The other car comes alongside and tries to ram the white Ford off the side of the road. Vincent speeds up even more.

The road in the mountains curves. The chase is on. The road gets steeper and steeper. Vincent uses the curve to get on the left side of the road and slows down. When the other car comes alongside on the right, Vincent accelerates and forces the car off the road. The mountainside is steep, and the other car goes over the side and falls into the ravine. Vincent speeds away.

Anthony cries, "Jesus, that was a close call."

Vincent asserts, "They shouldn't mess with a Dee-Troit driver. They are out to get us. I'm going to go back and confront them."

Anthony doesn't like that idea: "I think we should just get out of here. They have guns and we don't."

Vincent remarks, "They might be dead."

Vincent turns the white Ford around and heads back to the site where the other car went over. He stops the car and gets out. Anthony is frozen in the passenger seat. He wants nothing to do with this.

Vincent looks down the side of the mountain. The other car hit a tree at the bottom of the ravine. He sees one man running away from the car and a second man trying to climb up the steep side of the ravine. The driver is slumped over the wheel, either dead or badly injured. Vincent grabs a large branch lying on the ground and attacks the man climbing up the ravine. He slips and falls back down. Vincent gets back in the white Ford and starts up the engine.

Vincent has reached a conclusion: "We can't stay in Montreal tonight. Henri knows where we are staying and that our flight leaves tomorrow. They're all working together."

Anthony asks, "Then what should we do?"

Vincent thinks for a couple of minutes and then decides: "We have to trick them."

Vincent goes into contemplation. What does he know? He knows that the men in the black suits are out to get him, perhaps both him and Anthony. He knows it was their plan to take them out on the way back to Montreal. He knows that Henri knows where they are staying that night, and they all know the car they have been driving.

He is pretty sure that Henri is calling the shots and that he considers Vincent somehow a threat to his activities, his take-over. In that frame of mind, people will go to any means to get what they need.

These are the guys that play for keeps. These are the guys that killed Jimmy Hoffa, put him in the trunk of a car, and then put the car through the junk yard to be crushed. Pretty clever!

Vincent heard the story of Jacques diamond robbery, how he came out of the restaurant wearing a butcher coat, with a side of beef on the shoulder. Even the cops in the middle of the street didn't notice him. The people in town who knew him didn't notice him. He is getting into Jacques head. He has to outsmart them, to do the unpredictable.

Chapter 46

Vincent speeds along the highway, the white Ford winding through the mountains. He passes sign: MONTREAL 10 Km. He enters the city. Vincent observes: "Our motel is right by the airport, and we return this car to the airport. I've got an idea."

He pulls up in front of a Men's Clothing Store, stops the car and gets out. Anthony gets out, too, and follows Vincent into the store. Vincent walks up to the counter. The clerk asks: "How may I help you?"

Vincent responds, "I want to buy two of your male mannequins."

The clerk replies, "We don't sell those."

Vincent asks: "How much did you pay for them?"

The clerk has no idea: "I'm not sure. I'll have to ask the manager. He' s in the back "

The clerk goes into the back room. He comes out, followed by another man.

The manager looks Vincent in the eye and comments: "He says you want to but two of the mannequins. We don't sell those."

Vincent responds firmly: "I know it's an unusual request. I'll pay you double whatever they cost you."

The manager thinks for a moment and then says: "They were $20 apiece. I'll let you have two of them for $50."

Vincent takes out his wallet and counts out 50 American dollars. "I know our dollars are worth more than yours. This will cover it. Is it ok for us to undress the two mannequin in the window?"

The manager says: "We'll do it for you." He and the clerk go to the store window and remove two male mannequins. They take off the suits they are wearing.

Vincent shakes their hands. "Thank you. You have no idea how important this is for us."

The two brothers each pick up a mannequin and head out to the car. They put them in the back seat, laying them down on the floor. They get in the car.

"Ok," says Anthony. "Now what! Obviously you have a plan."

Vincent replies, "You'll see!"

He starts up the white Ford and drives to the airport. He stops in front of a car rental, parks, and gets out of the car. Anthony gets out, too, and follows Vincent into the car rental. The clerk asks: "Can I help you?"

Vincent replies: "I want to rent a car to drive one-way to Toronto."

The clerk asks: "How many days?"

Vincent replies: "Just two – today and tomorrow.

The clerk says, "I have a Chevy station wagon you can have for $30 a day, unlimited mileage."

Vincent agrees: "That works. What do you need from me?

The clerk says: "Credit card. Driver's license."

Vincent gives him the credit card and the driver's license, and the clerk types out the contract for Vincent to sign. Anthony goes to the coke machine. He asks, "Do you want a coke?"

Vincent says, "Sure." Anthony takes some change out of his pocket, puts it into the machine, and takes out two bottles of coke. He hands one to Vincent. Vincent signs the contract and the credit card bill. The clerk gives him the carbon copy and a map of Toronto showing where the car is to be returned.

The clerk opens the map and spreads it out. He points to a spot on the map: "You return it right by the airport. Here's where it is."

Vincent says, "That's great. Can I have the keys?"

The clerk takes a set of keys from the peg over his desk, and he motions to Vincent and Anthony to follow him out into the parking lot. The three of them go out to the black station wagon. The clerk goes over the exterior of the vehicle, looking for dents. Then he hands Vincent the keys.

Vincent shakes his hand and remarks, "Thank you. You have been very helpful."

Vincent hands Anthony the keys to the white Ford. He instructs him: "You drive the other car. Follow me to the motel."

Anthony still doesn't know the plan, but he does what he is told. Vincent pulls ahead of Anthony, and they go out the drive and down the street to the Holiday Inn. They chose this hotel because it is so close to the airport. Vincent pulls into the parking lot and parks the car. Anthony pulls up next to him and parks. They both get out of the cars and head for the Lobby. By now it is late afternoon.

The clerk at the front desk asks: "May I help you?"

Vincent replies, "You have a reservation for Vincent Pascal for one night."

The clerk looks into the reservation book and confirms: "Yes. You are in room 126."

Vincent plans ahead: "We are leaving early tomorrow morning for the airport. I would like to pay you now. We won't be charging anything to our room."

The clerk fills out the bill. "Are you putting it on a credit card?

Vincent says, "No. We'll pay cash."

The clerk says, "That will be $40."

Anthony says, "I will pay my half." He takes a $20 bill out of his wallet. Vincent also takes out a $20 bill.

Vincent tells the clerk: "These are American dollars. They're worth a little more, but you just keep the difference."

The clerk asks, "Where did you park?"

Vincent says, "We parked right by the entrance to the Lobby."

The clerk gives directions: "So when you go out the door, you will want to get in your car and drive around to the other side of the motel. Room 126 is just inside of the back entrance."

The clerk hands Vincent the key to the room. He and Anthony head for the door. Just before he exits, Vincent pauses and looks back over his shoulder at the clerk: "A couple of fellas are coming to meet us here. You can just send them to our room."

Anthony is surprised. He asks: "So, now what? What was that about?"

Vincent replies: "I'm expecting us to be followed. We're going to put the mannequins in the bed and head for Toronto in the station wagon. We'll leave the white Ford parked by the back entrance."

Anthony responds excitedly: "Damn! You're way ahead of me."

They each get into a car and drive around to the back of the motel.

Chapter 47

Vincent and Anthony pull up by the back entrance and park. They both get out of their cars. Vincent opens the trunk of the white Ford and takes out the suitcases. He puts them in the back of the black station wagon. He wants to get the lay of the land.

Vincent says, "Let's go in and find the room before we take in the mannequins." They head toward the back entrance of the Holiday Inn.

They find the room, actually just inside the entrance and the first left down the hall. Vincent opens the door: "Ok. Let's use the bathroom, and then we'll bring in the mannequins. It's just as well that it's starting to get dark. We won't be observed."

When they return to the parking lot, Anthony unlocks the white car and opens the back door. Each of the men lifts out a mannequin. No need to lock the Ford now. They have taken everything out of it. They proceed to the entrance and to the room. Vincent opens the door and gives instructions: "We'll put the mannequins in the bed and cover them up."

He pulls down the covers, and they each place a mannequin in the bed, lying on the side with faces downward. They pull up the covers. Vincent puts the key to the room on the dresser, and they head out the door.

When they get back to the parking lot, Vincent says, "Leave the keys in the Ford on the floor. The motel will be able to get the name of the car rental from the paper work in the cubbyhole."

Anthony does as he is told. Vincent gets into the driver's seat of the station wagon, Anthony gets in, and they drive out of the parking lot. They are on their way to Toronto.

Within half an hour of their departure, two men in black suits are standing in front of the clerk in the lobby of the Holiday Inn. One of them asks: "We were supposed to meet Vincent Pascal here tonight. Has he checked in yet?"

The clerk replies, "Yes, he and another man checked in. They are in room 126. Do you want me to call them?"

The other man says, "No, we'll just go to the room and meet them."

The clerk comments: "They checked in quite a while ago. They said they were leaving early in the morning for the airport. They may be asleep."

The first man says, "We'll go see. Which way is the room."

The clerk shows them the layout of the motel: "Just drive around to the back on the other side and park by the back entrance. 126 is just to the left down the hall."

The second man says, "Thank you. Appreciate your help."

The clerk replies, "Not a problem."

The two men get into their car to drive to the back of the motel. The first one says, "There's the white Ford. We know they're in there."

They go in the back entrance, turn left to find 126. The second man, bigger than the first, hits the door with his shoulder to force it open. The door swings open to reveal two people sleeping in the bed. The first man shoots the sleeping bodies, and the second man closes the door after them as they leave. They head out to the parking lot.

The first one says, "That was a lot easier than I expected. Pays them back for what happened in the mountains today."

Vincent and Anthony are well on their way to Toronto. Henri and his "committee" of three have all returned to Montreal. Catherine, Joseph and Renee were delivered to the airport on time for their flight, and Frank has been left waiting for his flight to Germany.

Henri's work with the family is concluded, except for Vincent, and they are taking care of him and his brother that night at the Holiday Inn. Good thing Vincent mentioned that's where they are staying. They expected to get it done on the highway as a car accident, but it didn't work out. There was an accident, the wrong fatalities. Henri has no attachment to anyone. He has only one intention: the takeover.

The four men meet the next day in the Conference Room of the Mt. Tremblant Holding Company. They are all seated at a conference table. Henri has a document in front of him. He passes copies to the other three men.

Henri begins: "We haven't been able to find a will. The attorney for the Holding Company doesn't have one. It looks like Jacques thought he had everything all wrapped up under his entire control and didn't need one."

One of the men asks, "What happened when Frenchie and Hungarian Joe went down in that plane?"

Henri replies: "Jacques had insurance policies on both of them, with himself as the beneficiary. In fact, he has insurance policies on all of us with the Holding Company as the beneficiary. This document says that if any of the principals is deceased, his portion is controlled by Jacques, as head of the Holding company."

A second man comments: "That means that Jacques collected the insurance from Frenchie and Hungarian Joe and then took over their shares in the Holding Company. We didn't know it would work that way when we took them out."

Henri says, "So here's how I see it. The four of us will assume the principal shares, and we have decision making power over the other shareholders."

A third man asks, "What about the widow? Can't she claim Jacques' position?"

Henri replies, "She doesn't know anything. She's just a young girl. And she's a Mohawk. They don't have any rights."

Another one comments: "I heard Jacques' Father ask where his money is. Evidently Jacques owed him money."

Henri responds: "Don't worry about the old man. The one that worried me was the oldest son, but we handled that last night. We take the Company with all of the properties. We divide it into five parts. One part is divided up and split among the sixteen guys. We each take one-fifth for ourselves."

The first man to speak asks, "Where's the cash from the insurance payments?"

Henri says, "I'm working on that. I haven't found it yet. Jacques sure thought he had it all. Any of us could have been next. We took care of that. The Doctor didn't have a clue. Cause of death: heart attack."

The second man asks: "Don't we need to take care of the widow."

The third man replies, "Leave that up to me."

Chapter 48

Vincent and Anthony are at LAX (Los Angeles International) waiting for their luggage to come down the ramp. They are greeted by a middle-aged woman and man who have come to pick them up. Shannon is now in her late '40s. Her hair is still red, with a little help, but she has plumped up significantly from the shapely, voluptuous young woman she was at 15. The brothers are relieved to be safely back in California and grateful to be met by their mother and step-father.

Shannon can't hold back her curiosity: "Well, how was it? Will you get an inheritance?"

Vincent replies, "It was a very strange funeral, with 20 of his closest friends in black suits. They tried to kill us on the way to the airport."

Anthony chimes in: "Forget the inheritance. We're lucky to be alive."

Vincent adds: "It's a long story. We'll fill you in on the way home. There were lots of things we didn't understand, other things we suspected. He had a child bride and two little boys. There's money, but I don't think the family will to get any of it. I have a friend who's an attorney with connections in Montreal. I am going to have him put out some feelers, but I don't expect much. These are people who cover their tracks."

On the ride home, Vincent edits the story. He and Anthony experienced this together, but their perceptions are different. Anthony's memory of their father is very vague. Jacques didn't spend time with him as he did with Vincent. Vincent's childhood memories are still vivid. The one seared in his memory is Shannon's beating. But there are others, all exciting for a child and characteristic of Jacques' unique flair for creating his own reality on the fringe of what was legal and accountable.

As young as he was, Vincent knew he shouldn't tell. He never told Shannon about the men in the pig sty, the storm that hit the slaughter house, shooting out the windows of the hotel, the pheasant hunting. Actually Jacques took him along with him quite often, and he liked being with his father, riding in the truck. That's probably why he kept his "adventures" secret.

The funeral had actually stoked these memories, especially his conversations with James Murray. He came to realize that Jacques didn't really change after he went to Montreal. He was just more of himself in a larger venue with greater possibilities. This was between Vincent and Jacques. No one in his family could comprehend it. That is the prerogative of the first child.

Anthony and Frank didn't go to the farm. Joseph and Catherine were only interested in Vincent, and he is the one who spent time at the farm. Once Joseph had called Vincent "Jacques" when he was driving the tractor, and Vincent had spun the wheels and cried out vehemently: "Don't ever do that again. I'll leave and never come back." Shannon had slipped and called him Jacques, too, and he had reprimanded her.

But there was Jacques, lying in the coffin, looking just like Vincent. Vincent does not mention that to Shannon. He does not tell her about the deaths of Frenchie and Hungarian Joe. She would remember that Vincent knew them, too. He tells her Joseph passed out when he saw his son in the coffin. He tells her about the mansion, the young wife, the two little boys, the men in the black suits, the huge wreath, the kiss on both cheeks, the chase on the highway. He does not tell her about the mannequins in the Holiday Inn. She would know that was just the sort of stunt Jacques would pull.

Vincent knows the limits of Shannon's mental capacity. Some people are just smarter than other people. Vincent is smarter than Anthony and Frank. Vincent is smarter than Shannon. Mick can keep up with Vincent, so can Joseph. Joseph only went to the fourth grade, but he farms and sells his products better than his brothers. A farmer has to be a good farmer and also a businessman. Jacques probably got his smarts from Joseph and his grit from Catherine.

Latonya's youth reminded him of Shannon's when she married Jacques. But Shannon was only sixteen, and he brought her home to a chicken coop. He should have kept his pants zipped. Latonya must have been in her early twenties. That makes a big difference. Latonya had worked in the family business. Vincent observed her run that house, instruct the servants, make arrangements, conduct herself with dignity even in her confusion about the men in the black suits. There really is no comparison. So why is he making it.

Vincent knows he is not the same person who left for the funeral. If anything, he understands himself a little better. Some of Jacques' genes could account for his getting into trouble at St. Patrick's, his "worldiness" that got him dumped from the Brotherhood, his quick promotions at U.S. Gypsum, his dirty tricks and practical jokes in the Army, even his persistence to get his degree, all those years part time while he worked and was in the Army. His determination to get his education was similar to Jacques' determination to become a bush pilot.

He also is pretty sure there's nothing for him in Canada. If he had any doubts, the chase sealed it. He does call his attorney friend to contact the lawyer in Montreal. The scared doctor when he asked about the autopsy, the scared priest who performed the funeral service, they were both taking orders. When he hears from him, the response is abrupt and final: "My friend says he wouldn't touch this case with a ten-foot pole. You saw the players. They play for keeps. Better forget it and be glad you're not dead, too."

Vincent is glad he's here in California, not in Saint Jovite. His wife isn't as pretty as Latonya, but then few women he has ever met are as beautiful. Her beauty will not save her. As he is thinking these thoughts, a car is driving alongside the lake in Saint Jovite, toward Jacques' mansion, up the drive. It parks by the front door. Latonya's parents go up to the front door, ring the bell, expecting to see the servant.

When no one answers, they ring again. Latonya's father tries the knob, and the door opens. They enter the foyer, look down the hall. Two suitcases are by the door. He calls out: "Latonya, we're here. Where are you?"

They move into the living room and see the boys playing on the floor. They look up. Over their heads, Latonya hangs from a beam in the living room, fully dressed, wearing a light coat and hat, dressed for travel. Their shrieks reverberate through the house and can be heard as far away as Saint Jovite and the Murray's home at the far end of the lake. Vincent's premonition has been realized, a grotesque completion for the heirs of the missing spoke.

The Butcher from McGregor

ABOUT THE AUTHOR

Adrian Windsor is the author of *Seven Tools to Transform Genius into Practical Power* and *Get Off the Hampster Wheel*. She served as the ghost writer for *Gorby 2 Audacious Imposter* and *The Guy Who Got Trump*. She holds a B.A., M.A., and Ph.D. from the University of Michigan and has had a long career in academia and business.